I0551501

Blackout Protocol

Blackout Protocol

Written by

D. Skvarek

2025

First Edition: 2025

ISBN 979-8-9933345-0-9

Vivifica Studios, LLC
4381 North 75th St, Suite 201
Scottsdale, AZ 85251

Dedication

For the little bird with the bow.

Contents

Chapter 1
The Awakening

"We're going to be late, honey!" Donovan called out as he adjusted his shirt and jacket in the mirror. He had always been strict when it came to being prompt, or looking sharp for that matter. He didn't really know why, but it didn't matter why because the result was he was never late. Almost.

"What earrings should I wear with this dress?" Donovan's wife, Kathy, called out from the master bathroom. He took a deep breath and replied the best answer he could come up with.

"Whichever you want, honey. I'm sure it will look fine."

Wrong answer.

"Look fine?" Kathy asked, as she emerged from the bathroom in her red, knee-length dress, black stockings and heels. "So I just look fine now?"

"That's not what I meant. I meant any of your earrings will go with your outfit... and look, *great*," Donovan tried to cover. Kathy raised an eyebrow at him at shot lasers from her eyes through his skull. Or at least that what it looked like to Donovan as he mustered an innocent smile.

"Which... ones?" Kathy said, holding up two pair in each hand.

"The ones in your right hand," Donovan glanced down at his watch.

"There are two pair in my right hand, dear." Kathy's eyes burned with the fury of a thousand suns. Donovan took another breath, knowing that if he didn't pick soon, and pick correctly, they would be late.

"Diamond studs," he said, pointing.

"Perfect, thank you!" Kathy beamed and disappeared back into the bathroom, leaving Donovan to breathe a sigh of relief and check his watch again. Much to his pleasure, Kathy appeared again moments later, wearing a pair of thin gold hoops in her ears. Donovan started to protest but thought better of it, and escorted his wife out the door of their hotel room.

The Atlantis Hotel was fairly new to the Las Vegas Strip, and as such it attracted newer, classier shows than some that had been playing in Vegas for years on end. It was also one of the more expensive hotel casinos on the Strip, and sought the high rolling, high spending type of clientele. While Donovan wasn't exactly a wealthy man, his commercial real estate business had done well, and Kathy was a well respected psychiatrist. Between the two of their incomes, spending a lavish weekend in Las Vegas wasn't going to break the bank.

Kathy had insisted Donovan forgo the tie, and told him a nice shirt and jacket would be just fine for a Las Vegas show. She was proven right when they arrived at their showroom in the hotel, and found more than half the guests wearing shorts and sandals, or some other form of casual wear.

"It's Vegas, dear," she had told him. "They don't care how you dress as long as you leave your wallet on the table."

"*I* care how I dress," Donovan had retorted. "Let the others dress like slobs if they want. After all, looking dapper is my calling card. It's my specialty."

As the two gave their tickets and started towards their private table, a huge rotating image of their entertainer for the night hovered over the stage. He smiled, looking out over the crowd with his unseeing eyes, then his image exploded into millions of pixels and formed his name in gold.

Marc Julien the Mentalist

Donovan looked up at the words dancing over the stage as he unbuttoned his jacket and took his seat. Seeing a comedy hypnotist wasn't his idea, but Kathy's, and he wasn't too thrilled about the whole thing. Still, it made her happy and he figured he would have fun with it. The show was supposed to be entertaining, and for what the tickets had cost him, Donovan hoped it wouldn't disappoint.

The lights fell as the audience grew quiet, then suddenly an explosion of fireworks from the stage and loud music filled the showroom. From the smoke on the stage and amid laser lights came the man himself, dressed in black slacks, alligator boots, a plain white button up shirt and a flashy, red velvet jacket. The audience cheered, Kathy whistled, and Donovan slow-clapped.

"Welcome ladies and gentlemen! I am Marc Julien the Mentalist, and I can read your mind!" He said with a smile and one hand on his temple. "Okay, okay, maybe not. But I can convince you to do some really embarrassing things they'll be talking about at the office all year!"

The audience roared.

"Hypnosis is the ancient art of reaching deep into the subconscious and unlocking the hidden potential of your mind. Through the proper training, and with time a hypnotist can help you stop smoking, put the bottle down, even unlock the ability to heal your body. Which is exactly why I'm going to use it tonight to make some lucky fools cluck like a chicken."

More raucous laughter from the audience. Donovan gave Kathy a look out of the corner of his eye. She was laughing with the rest, so he settled back a bit and tried to enjoy himself.

"Of course this show is all about audience participation, so for the next ninety minutes I'm going to ask some of you to join me on stage, but most of you to enjoy with cheers, jeers, and suggestions."

Donovan leaned over the small table and spoke to Kathy loud enough for her to hear over the audience.

"Who would honestly subject themselves to that kind of humiliation?" He asked.

"Oh good!" Marc shouted and strode to the edge of the stage. "We have our first volunteer!" A spotlight lit up and quickly crossed the stage to where Marc stood, a few feet away from Donovan and Kathy's table. The light then centered on the couple, as Kathy's eyes lit up with surprise, and Donovan slowly looked up at the hypnotist.

"And who is this happy couple here?" Marc asked, squatting down to get closer.

"Uh," Donovan began, "we're just here for the show."

"Well I'd hope so, because those seats you have were *not* cheap. What's your name, sir?"

"I, uh…"

"Donovan, his name is Donovan," Kathy leaned forward and blurted out.

"Donovan, that sounds very official. Well how about it, Donovan? Will you be the first to subject yourself to public humiliation?" Marc grinned wide and held out a microphone towards the stunned Donovan.

"I was just… uh," Donovan looked over at Kathy who was beaming at him. Then she leaned towards the microphone and announced in her sweetest voice.

"My husband would love to be your first victim."

"Everyone give Donovan a round of applause!" Marc shouted as he stepped back and made his way towards the center of the stage. Two stagehands quickly rushed the small table and offered their help to get Donovan onto the stage, which he immediately declined. He stood and buttoned his jacket, as the audience cheered, and made his way to the stairs on the side of the stage.

"As our subject joins me, I want to give a little background here," Marc started, while stools were rushed onto the stage by stagehands dressed all in black. "Everyone, yes *everyone* can be hypnotized. In fact, you do it every night when you go to sleep. That doesn't mean that everyone *will* be hypnotized on stage tonight."

Donovan reached the hypnotist and stood back a little, not wanting to crowd the man or take up anymore attention than he really should.

"Every person that joins me here must be willing to allow me into their subconscious. I cannot *make* anyone do anything, I can only give suggestions once they are in a relaxed and calm state. Remember, I'm not a psychic or a mind reader, I merely make suggestions." Marc stepped backwards, then turned his back to the crowd and pressed a small button on his belt, muting the microphone.

"Just go with it, relax, we're all here to have a good time," he said quietly to Donovan, who gave a single nod and put on his best fake smile.

"Now, we'll start with some very simple commands to get him into a hypnotic state. Donovan if would please take out your wallet." Donovan paused a moment, then shrugged and pulled his wallet from his back pocket. "Very good, now please open your wallet and tell me, are you carrying cash?"

Donovan did as he was asked, then nodded and spoke up as loud as he could. "Yes, I've got some cash on me."

"Good, good. If you have a one dollar bill, please remove it and hand it to me," Marc said while the audience waited patiently. Donovan flipped through his cash, pulled out a single and handed it over to the hypnotist who held it up in the air, then folded it and placed it in his pocket.

"Excellent, good work so far. Now, Donovan, please remove a one hundred dollar bill and hand it to me."

Donovan started to pull out the bill but paused and gave the man a suspicious look. The audience responded with laughter and Marc held up his hands in defeat.

"It was worth a try!" He laughed and pulled the bill from his pocket, waving it to the audience. "He must be already half under and I haven't done anything!"

More laughter, as Marc handed the single back and offered a stool to Donovan. Feeling a bit foolish already, he stuffed the bill in his coat pocket and glanced down at Kathy, who was smiling wide. There was something about seeing his wife happy and having fun that made it worth the while, so he sat on the stool, loosened his collar, and looked Marc in the eyes.

"All right, let's see what you can do," Donovan said with a smile.

"Now that's the right attitude!" Marc placed hand on Donovan's shoulder and raised his other hand near his face. "Now I want you to focus on my voice, and nothing else. Nothing else in the world exists right now but my voice. You hear the sound, the sound of my voice making sound but you don't hear other sounds. The stillness of the sound my voice makes makes you relaxed and at peace. My voice makes you peaceful, and peace is what you want when you hear my voice make a sound."

Donovan stared at Marc's hand, he felt the hand on his shoulder, and he focused as best he could on Marc's voice. But just the sound of his voice began to change, blend, as though the words he was speaking were getting jumbled.

"...voice sound makes peace sound voice when you calm voice makes makes sound voice focus sound..."

Donovan blinked, shook his head and tried to look away from Marc's hand. But he couldn't. His hand was interesting. No, that wasn't the right term at all. It was *mesmerizing.* Donovan wanted to reach out and touch the hand but his own hands wouldn't work. They were...

Hot.

Real hot.

Like fire.

Donovan swore he felt the stool move under him but it couldn't be, he was sitting firm. In the peripheral of his vision he saw his wife, smiling. But then she wasn't. She was looking at him intently, worried, scared even.

Marc's hand started to close, his middle finger and thumb pressed together in an odd fashion, like they were dancing, or about to dance. Donovan thought that would be nice, dancing right now, but he had to focus on the sound of something. What was it?

"And sleep!" Marc announced, and snapped his fingers.

Donovan closed his eyes, and the calming sound of the voice suddenly changed. No longer was it calm, relaxing, or soothing. It was something else entirely. There were multiple voices as well. Hundreds of them. All at once making the same sound together like a song. But no, they weren't singing, it was a weird sound, a bad sound.

Donovan closed his eyes tighter, trying to focus on the sound of all the voices, when suddenly he recognized it. It wasn't music or a song he was hearing. He heard the audience.

They were screaming.

Chapter 2
Dazed and Confused

Donovan opened his eyes slowly, groggily, like waking up from a weird dream or having too much to drink the night before. The first thing he saw was his hands, clenched into fists and slightly shaking. He stared at them like he had never seen them before, like they weren't even his. It took a full minute of staring at them before he could open his fists, and once he did, the rest of his body seemed to relax. All except his head. His head was pounding all of a sudden, like the worst headache he'd had in his life. He groaned and tried to stand and the pain increased.

"...mister O'Connell... sir..."

"...hands where we..."

"...turn around and..."

There were voices all around him, but none of them were making any sense. He managed to look to the left and could make out blurry images that looked like people, but people usually weren't blurry. He looked to the right and it was the same, several men it looked like but it was hard to tell with the blazing light in his eyes.

The light.

Like stage lights.

He was still on stage, but that couldn't be right either, the last thing he remembered was sitting across from Kathy at the show. Some kind of show in some place where she wouldn't let him wear a tie for some reason.

Donovan shook his head and looked to the left again, the people were slowly getting closer, so he raised a hand to try and motion that everything was fine. Suddenly they all jumped back, like they were afraid of him or something. He found that extremely odd, and to his right he could hear more commotion and words that didn't make sense. They all sounded so panicked and almost afraid of him.

"It's ok... just give me... I need to wake up just... where's Kathy?" Donovan managed to mumble out. It sounded normal in his mind, but the people on the left looked at each other like he was speaking a foreign language.

"Mr. O'Connell, I need you to put your hands on your head," one of the people said.

"My head?" Donovan replied. That didn't make any sense either, but he thought he'd give it a try. He raised his arms higher than they needed to be and rested his hands on his forehead. His head hurt so much that the room spun the moment he touched it. He had been aiming for the top of his head but the forehead would have to work. In an instant he was swarmed and thrown to the ground on his face, the people yanked his hands behind his back and began cuffing them.

"What are you doing? Where's Kathy?" Donovan asked again, but no one seemed interested in answering him. He was pulled to his feet by several men, and the stage lights hit him in the eyes, prompting him to shut his eyes tight. Behind his eyelids he saw chairs flying into the air, even as people sat on them, shoes, purses, then the tables went soaring back as well.

Donovan shook his head and strained to open his eyes, willing them to focus this time. That's when he saw it. The showroom was in complete disarray. Tables like the one he and Kathy had been sitting at were everywhere, one even stuck into the ceiling of the showroom. Paramedics were working on multiple guests and there were chairs laid out in spray patterns like a truck had ran through the crowd.

Several trucks.

"What… what happened? Where's Kathy? Where's my wife?" Donovan asked frantically.

"Get him out of here, before it happens again," one man to the side said. Donovan looked up and saw the man was a police officer. In fact, all the men surrounding him were, about a dozen of them, with at least six carrying large rifles. Donovan focused on the name tag as best he could.

"Officer… Bradley," he said. "Please, where's my wife?" Donovan asked pleadingly.

"I don't know, son," the man said, his voice deep and booming and powerful, but somehow relaxing at the same time. "But you better pray she isn't one of them poor folks." Bradley pointed towards the crowd of moaning and wailing people among the devastation in the audience.

Donovan didn't understand any of what was going on, even as they escorted him out of the hotel and into a secure S.W.A.T. truck, where he was surrounded by the heavily armed police officers. He tried to think hard about what he was seeing versus what he remembered, but all he could come up with was the voice of the hypnotist lulling him into a relaxed state. He thought it better to say nothing for the short trip to the police station. He'd have to call his attorney, and hope to get ahold of Kathy somehow. She would at least be able to tell him what happened after he fell asleep, or whatever it was that happened to him.

Hours ticked by while he sat in an interrogation room alone, cuffed to a metal table that was bolted to the concrete floor. Nobody had come to see him, asked him any questions or even if he needed a drink of water or to go to the bathroom. Which he did. The frustration was starting to build and he fully intended to give the next person he saw an earful once the door finally opened. Whenever that would be.

No phone call. No lawyer. No word from his wife.

Donovan closed his eyes tight, trying to rest, relax, sleep, anything, but it was all for nothing. He lay his head down on the cold metal table and something flashed before his eyes. Jerking, he sat up with a start, confused at what he just saw behind his eyelids. He cautiously closed them again, and lay his head back on the table, when it happened once more.

Like a memory, but from a time and place he didn't know, nor had ever been. He saw white walls and men and women in lab coats wearing protective eyewear, all smiling at him at he passed. There was a giant screen with readouts he didn't understand, and an observation window adjacent to the screen. Donovan approached the window and peered down below into what appeared to be an open room with random piece of furniture scattered about.

And someone.

The door to the interrogation room opened with a loud clank, causing Donovan to sit up suddenly. In walked Lieutenant Bradley with two other men in suits that didn't look too pleased, but also a little nervous to see Donovan.

"You can't hold me like this. I have rights, you know. I want to talk to my lawyer, and my wife," Donovan demanded, as the three men sat down across the table from him. Without a word Bradley placed a file down on the table, it was fairly thin and Donovan could see his name on the tab.

Donovan took a moment to examine Bradley. He was an older black man, heavy and tall, but looked like he could

Page 12

handle himself despite his weight. He reminded Donovan of those strong men competitors who didn't look like they were made of muscle, more like they had spent too much time at the taco bar. But they could lift a car well enough. His white trimmed mustache beguiled his age, and he breathed like someone who had just ascended a flight of stairs. Several flights of stairs.

Bradley crossed his fingers and leaned forward on the table, staring Donovan in the eyes. He was tired, and about a decade older than Donovan in his late fifties, but the job had gotten to him, and he obviously wasn't looking forward to whatever was going on. The men at his right and left were very obviously not local, most likely federal agents, but from which agency Donovan had no idea. However, they also didn't want to be there. That made all four of them.

"Mister O'Connell," Bradley started in a deep rumbling voice, "it's late, I'm tired, and these two gentlemen here are as well. I'm sure you'd like to get back to your life too, but see, we have a problem." Bradley opened the file and turned it around to face Donovan. Inside were bank records, employment papers, a copy of his driver's license, and various other documents identifying Donovan.

"Are you going to tell me, or do I have to guess?" Donovan asked, leaning forward to match Bradley's posture. The older man sat back rather quickly, as though intimidated, and cleared his throat.

"This is your life, Mr. O'Connell, but the problem is it's all fake," Bradley said with a certain degree of insecurity.

"Fake? What do you mean fake?" Donovan shot back.

"He means fraudulent," the man to the right of Bradley spoke up.

"This here is Security Agent Parker," Bradley said, pointing a thumb at the man. "He's with Homeland Security. And to my left is Special Agent Miller with the FBI. Unfortunately what you've done tonight constitutes as domestic terrorism. And with the added fraud—"

"Wait, what do you mean domestic terrorism?" Donovan interrupted. "What did I do? And what fraud?"

Agent Parker intertwined his fingers and leaned closer to Donovan. "That's what we're here to ascertain. What *did* you do? And more importantly, how did you do it and where is the weapon now?"

"What weapon!?" Donovan raised his voice which caused all three men to scoot back in their chairs, as though they were about to bolt from the room. Bradley turned towards the reflective glass window and held up a hand, obviously motioning whoever was on the other side that things were under control.

"Now Mr. O'Connell, I need you to keep yourself together, otherwise I'm going to have you sedated," Bradley said, his voice quivering.

"Please, I'm asking you, please tell me what happened and why I'm locked up here. What... happened... back... at the casino?" Donovan placed his hands flat against the table, trying to calm himself, but he felt the table itself vibrating under his palms. Bradley was the first to stand up from his chair, slowly, with his eyes fixed on Donovan's hands. Agent Miller was the next to get up, while Agent Parker sat stunned, watching the table vibrate.

The door opened suddenly, another officer stood in the doorway and cleared his throat.

"Lieutenant, his attorney is on the phone," the officer said.

"His attorney?" Bradley looked to Donovan, who looked back just as shocked. The table became still.

"How did he... never mind. Get him up and to the phones. He's got sixty seconds, not a moment more." Bradley strode out of the room, the two agents scurrying close behind. Three other officers entered and carefully restrained Donovan, who didn't resist in the least, then guided him to the phones.

Donovan waited for the officers to give him some space, then he lifted the receiver to his ear.

"Thomas? What the hell is going on?"

"Shut up and listen to me," came a man's voice on the other end. "You need to get out of there, and fast. I've arranged extraction but you have to do exactly what I say."

"Who is this? What are you talking about?" Donovan said in a whispered voice to avoid drawing suspicion from the waiting officers.

"Get out, and go to the South parking lot. There will be a pickup truck waiting," the voice said.

"Get out how? Tell me who you are," Donovan growled into the phone.

"If you want to get out of this alive, you'll do as I say. South parking lot, pickup truck. Ten minutes."

The line went dead. Donovan swallowed hard and pretended to still be listening for a few more seconds before faking the end of the call.

"Right. I'll see you in ten to fifteen minutes then. No don't worry I won't say anything else." He slowly hung up the receiver and turned to the officers. "He'll be here in ten to fifteen minutes," Donovan said, and shrugged. The officers quickly grabbed him by the arms and escorted him back to the interrogation room.

"I… don't believe it," Agent Parker said quietly to Bradley and Miller, as they stood behind the mirrored glass and watched Donovan. "We all saw that devastation. He's got a weapon somewhere, and Homeland will not let him go until he tells us where it is."

"We have jurisdiction here," Miller said. "Homeland can have what's left of him after the FBI are done."

"You're all forgetting this happened in my city, under my watch," Bradley said as calmly as he could muster. "Until I get answers, O'Connell is mine."

"This is a little over your pay grade, Lieutenant," Parker said with a smirk.

"Then you can call the mayor and get my pay grade raised, Agent Parker." Bradley quickly turned and left the room, heading back to the interrogation door. "Open the door, and have that sedative ready in case things go south," he commanded the two officers posted outside the door.

Donovan looked up as Bradley entered, the two suits quickly following behind.

"Look, I just spoke to my lawyer and—"

"Cut the crap, O'Connell," Bradley barked. "You may not realize this but you're in deep shit. I'm talking real deep. Both of these men here want to drag you out of here and put you in a hole where folks like us just disappear. You say your lawyer's coming? That's fine. But they want to take you places lawyers have never heard of. So give me something here, right now, and I'll hold off the jackals."

Donovan put his handcuffed hands flat on the table, and took a deep breath.

"I don't know what you want, Lieutenant. I don't know what happened at the casino. I was sitting with my wife and suddenly I'm on the stage with your police throwing me on the ground. That's it. That's all I know."

"That's not what the witnesses said. They said you went crazy. They said you," Bradley opened the file on the table and shook his head as he read the words. "You moved things with your mind," He looked up at Donovan with a raised eyebrow.

"I moved things with my mind?" Donovan scoffed. "What like, pencils and paperclips?"

"Like people," Bradley growled.

"You know that's impossible. That kind of thing doesn't happen," Donovan said as he leaned forward.

"How do you explain the chairs, the bodies, the tables?" Parker shot out. "How do you explain the dozens of dead people who just went to a show for a good time? You did that, O'Connell."

"I don't know what you're talking about," Donovan said, slapping his hands on the table.

"I think you do," Parker leaned forward. "I think you know exactly what you did. Tell us where the weapon is."

"Parker back off," Bradley insisted.

"Tell us where the weapon is or I'll put you in such a deep hole you'll beg to see the sun," Parker leaned forward even more.

"I don't know what you're talking about. I didn't do anything!" Donovan slapped the table again, as it began to vibrate in an unnatural way.

"Tell us! Where is the weapon?"

"Parker!" Bradley shouted.

"I told you," the table began to tremble violently under Donovan's hands. "I don't... know... anything!"

"Davis, get in here with that sedative!" Bradley shouted. "Hurry, dammit! Get in here!"

There was a commotion outside the room that Donovan could hear, and then the door burst open with a man and a woman, both wearing surgical gloves, though the man carried a stun baton and the woman had a syringe in her hand.

Donovan screamed and stood suddenly, as the metal table was ripped from the floor and flew across the room sideways, and pinned the two agents and Bradley to the opposite wall. Donovan's jaw dropped, and he looked down at his hands, which were still handcuffed, though the chain had been broken from the table.

"Agh! Don't stand there sedate him!" Bradley called out, as he tried to push the table off his body. It wouldn't budge.

Donovan held out his hands toward the other officers. "Please, I... I don't know what's happening here! Please don't come closer!"

The male officer nodded frantically while the woman backed away into the hallway and disappeared. A heartbeat later, the station alarm was sounded. Donovan hung his head and looked to where the other men were still pinned to the wall. He glanced down at his hands, when suddenly something changed. He couldn't quite place it, but he saw something, almost as though the air around his hand *bent*.

Reaching out towards the table, Donovan closed one fist slowly, and it was like he could feel the table even across the room. He carefully pulled his arm back just an inch, and the table fell to the floor, freeing the men from their binding. Donovan winced as his head throbbed with pain.

"I'm... I'm sorry I... I have no idea what's happening," Donovan said, then turned and quickly left the

Page 18

interrogation room. The hallway was filled with police heading in his direction, so he spun around and ran down the corridor the opposite way.

"Freeze!" An officer shouted from behind him, but he had no intention of staying there any longer. He ran as fast as he could through the station, his hands still cuffed together.

A gunshot rang out and echoed in the hallway, followed by another and another, but the pursuing officers were just far enough away and just around another corner, allowing Donovan to slip by. Until he ran into a long narrow hall with police waiting on the other end.

"Get your hands up now!" He heard someone shout as they blinded him with flashlights. Reluctantly, he raised his hands slowly until they were in line with his face. And there it was again, bent air near his hands, pulsating, like near invisible waves.

Donovan glanced to the left where a barred window overlooked the parking lot of the police station. He swallowed hard and gently turned towards the window.

"Please, I don't want to do this," he said.

"Then don't!" A different officer shouted. "We're three stories up, you're not going to like where you land!"

"No," Donovan said softly, "I'm not."

He pushed his hands against the air, against the black wall and window and rebar and glass and everything shattered outward as though a truck had crashed through the building. His head throbbed with pain that nearly blinded him for a moment, but he shook it off as best he could and stared at the freshly made exit. The flashlights that had been blinding him were pointed in all directions now, as the officers all ducked for cover once the wall exploded. Without a second thought,

Donovan flung himself through the opening, swinging his arms wildly to try and steer himself through the air.

At the last moment he thrust his hands down to brace his fall, but it didn't work. He crashed into the roof of a police van, shattering the windshield, and tumbled off onto the asphalt with a thud. The pain was very real, as he rolled onto his back and groaned out loud. But he couldn't lay there in agony, he needed to move and fast.

Getting to his feet was hard enough, much less hobbling across the parking lot towards a barbed-wire fence. He could hear voices, screams and shouts as officers poured out of the station in pursuit. He had no choice but to try again as he reached the fence.

He focused through the pain in his leg and hip and head, and grabbed the chain link with both hands. The strange sensation returned, and he almost thanked God for it, as the fence strained and stretched. Then it gave way, tearing just wide enough for Donovan to squeeze through, although ripping his pants in the process.

"Hey! Hey General!" He heard someone shout, just as the headlights of an old pickup truck lit up and covered him. "General! Hurry! Get in!" The voice said. Donovan didn't think twice, given that the full police force was nearly on him. He hobbled around to the passenger side of the truck, and opened the old squeaky door. Inside was a man near his own age, wearing a flannel shirt, worn bluejeans and a trucker's baseball hat.

"Who are you?" Donovan asked, trying to climb inside. The man reached over and grabbed Donovan by his lapel and hoisted him into the truck, then hit the gas pedal before the passenger door was even closed.

"You really made a m-m-mess out there, huh?" The man stuttered the last word and laughed out loud as the engine roared and he tore towards the edge of the city.

"Easy! Watch the road!" Donovan tried to sit upright but found it difficult as the truck swerved in and out of traffic.

"We have to g-get out of town fast," the man said. "That was fun though! It w-w-was just like you said it would be."

Donovan turned his head and examined the man the best he could in the strobing street lights that they passed so quickly.

"You have got to tell me what's going on here," Donovan pleaded. "Who are you? Are you the man on the phone? Do you know Kathy?"

"Kathy?"

"My wife."

"You have a wife?!" The man swerved again and chuckled once more. "I never thought you'd be married!"

"The road!"

"I don't know your wife. I just was watching and I ca-aaame to get you like you said," the man said calmly. "I'm Joe, remember?"

"No, I don't remember. I don't know you," Donovan said as he pressed his fingers into his temples and grimaced at the pain in his throbbing head, then looked into the side mirror to see if the cops had caught up yet.

"You will," Joe said with a smile on his face. The two of them drove in silence from then on, as the lights of the city faded behind them.

Chapter 3
W.M.D.

When he opened his eyes, Donovan found himself laying on a worn sofa, his slick attire replaced with oversized sweat pants and a hoodie. He sat up and groaned at the pain in his body, and especially his head. In fact the longer he sat there the more he realized that everything hurt. The details of the night before swirled in his mind like a soup, with images and noises and voices and...

"Ugh..." he moaned out loud as he cracked his neck from one side to the other. "Did I... fall onto a car?" He said, mostly to himself, as he rubbed his neck.

"Yeah you di-did," a voice said from the other room. Donovan stood up fast, too fast, and his head spun, forcing him to sit back down on the sofa.

"Who's there?" He demanded.

"It's just me," the voice said.

"Who's me? Show yourself, I'm armed!"

"No you're not. Well, kinda. But not. But kinda," the voice trailed off, then in walked Joe, the same flannel shirt and jeans as the night before, except now he also dawned a flower-print apron, and held a sizzling pan in one hand.

"You! You're from last night! The truck... I... I can't really remember," Donovan held both palms to his forehead as though that might help him jog his addled brain.

Then it came crashing back, like an ebbed wave roaring onto a dry shore.

He saw clearly in his mind the police station, moving the table, running down the hall and *somehow* blowing a hole open in the building. Then there was the fall. He had tried something to brace his fall, what was it? But he hit the top of the cruiser hard, and rolled off. Then there was a truck...

"You were in the truck," he said matter of factly, though mostly to himself and not to the other man.

"Bingo," Joe said, as he slinked back into the kitchen. Donovan stood from the couch and moved to join him in the kitchen, who was busy making a delicious smelling breakfast.

"Joe. You're Joe, right?" Donovan asked cautiously.

"Y-y-yes I am," Joe stuttered.

"What am I doing here? Wait, does that mean... last night actually happened?" Donovan leaned back against a counter to keep his balance, as the pain in his body combined with the shock of this new revelation made him want to collapse onto the floor.

"Yes," Joe said plainly. "It all happened. I brought you here, because you told me to," Joe flipped the eggs in the pan and glanced at Donovan with a smile. "I always do what I'm to-told because I'm a good soldier. That's what you always said. I'm a good soldier."

"I always said?" Donovan shook his head. "Ok look, I don't know you Joe, and thanks for helping me last night and all, but I need to get home and check on my wife. And I need to figure out what in the world is going on here."

Joe shook his head.

"You have to stay, sir. You told me not to let you g-g-go if I found you," Joe said, without looking at Donovan.

"I've never met you before last night, so that's impossible. I didn't tell you anything."

"You d-did. You told me," Joe insisted.

"You know what? Fine, thanks again but I'm leaving," Donovan said as he turned to exit the kitchen.

"No! You have to stay!" Joe reached out his right hand and swung it to the side. Suddenly Donovan staggered backwards as though some unseen force and grabbed him by the shoulder and jerked him. He regained his footing and stared at Joe with startled eyes.

"What… did you… just do?" Donovan asked slowly.

"I'm sorry, sir, but you can't. I was told…"

"Answer me. What did you just do," Donovan said again, with his head lowered towards Joe. Joe looked away and swallowed hard.

"I T.K. pushed you," he said quietly.

"You what?"

"T.K. I did a telekin-kin-kin…" Joe stuttered and finally gave up trying to say the word.

"Telekinesis?" Donovan asked, his eyes wide. Joe merely nodded and dumped the eggs onto a nearby plate.

"Breakfast is ready," he said, and took the plate to a small rickety table where places were set for two people.

"Okay, you're going to have to run that by me again. You pushed me, with your mind?" Donovan chuckled a little and shook his head. "That's not possible."

"Sure it is. You do it all the time," Joe said, as he pulled several strips of bacon from another pan and placed them on the plates at the table.

"*I* do it?"

"You do it. All the time. You did last night. At the hotel show and in the puh-puh-police station," Joe took off the apron and took his seat at the table, then pointed at the other chair. Donovan slowly sat down across from him, and shook his head.

"What do you mean, I did it at the hotel show?" He asked slowly.

"Chairs, tables, people. You moved them, all of th-them with your mind. You do it all the time. It's your sp-sp-specialty." Joe smiled, then grabbed a fork and started to dig into his breakfast. Donovan steepled his fingers and rested his elbows on the table, trying to comprehend what this man was telling him about what had happened the night before.

"How do you know what happened last night?" He finally asked after a minute of silence.

Joe swallowed a large bite of eggs and nodded with a smile. "I saw it. I saw you. I didn't know you were b-b-back so I was happy to see you. Now we can finish everything you s-s-aid we would because you're back."

"You *saw* it? What did you see?" Donovan was becoming impatient with Joe, but he tried still to keep his cool. This man might be the only one who could tell him what was going on, since the police obviously didn't have any answers.

"I work there. I clean floors and trash after shows. I didn't know you were there until I heard noises. I came to see and you were on s-stage with the mind guy. Boom! Tables into the roof! I was so happy to see you doing your thing again!" Joe beamed and shoveled another large bite into his smiling mouth.

Donovan ran his hands through his hair and groaned, then looked up at Joe who seemed perfectly at peace with the chaos of the night before.

"Look, I appreciate your help, but I need to go. I need to find my wife and figure all this out and—"

"They're looking for you," Joe interrupted.

"Who? Who's looking for me?"

"The cops," Joe said, and waved his hand at an old tube television that sat on the counter. It turned on to a news station where Donovan's picture was prominently displayed in the corner.

"The search continues for a Las Vegas man accused of setting off a bomb at a casino show last night, which left over twenty wounded, and three dead," a reporter on the screen said, as she stared grimly into the camera.

"The man, identified as Donovan O'Connell, was taken into custody, but then escaped from police, and is now at large."

"This can't be happening," Donovan said, as he stood from his chair and stared at the television. "A *bomb?*"

"Police are asking for any leads regarding the whereabouts of O'Connell, but are advising citizens not to engage as he is considered armed, and extremely dangerous. Back to you." The reporter finished, and the scene changed. Donovan sat down hard and glanced up once more at the television. His eyes shot open wide as he noticed Lieutenant Bradley about to give a press conference, and large poster to his side with Donovan's picture on it. Just then the television turned off.

"Wait! Turn that back on!" Donovan shouted, as he jumped up and tried turning nobs and switches to turn the television back on.

"Oh those don't work," Joe said. "You have to, you know, whoosh, do the TK thing," he waved his hand around like he was washing a window.

"Whoosh thing? Please just turn it back on!"

"Do the...the thing," Joe smiled and encouraged him as though he were teaching a toddler to walk. Donovan growled in frustration, but turned to face the television and held out a hand. He swiped his hand across the screen a few times, but to no avail, so he tried waving more quickly like Joe had done, but nothing happened.

"It's not working!" He growled.

"That's cause you're just w-w-waving air. Your mind does it, not your hand!" Joe laughed, mouth full of food, as he enjoyed watching Donovan struggle. With a snort and a sigh, Donovan turned back to the the television frustrated, and waved his hand quickly again.

"Turn on, dammit!" He shouted. The screen came to life just in time for Donovan to catch the weather report. "No... no no no!"

"Why do you need to see the cop?" Joe asked, as Donovan pressed his forehead against the television screen.

"Because that's who arrested me. He might have an-swers about what happened to me." He said, rolling his head on the screen to look at Joe.

"He doesn't know w-what happened," Joe said flatly.

"How do you know that, Joe?" Donovan asked through gritted teeth.

Joe chuckled. "You're like a baby, General. You were never this fun before."

"Why do you keep calling me 'General'? Please I just want to find my wife and figure this out," Donovan said and sank to the floor. Joe got up from the table and sat down the on the floor, crossed legged, with some effort then reached over and patted Donovan on the back with a firm hand.

"You don't remember. But you will. I know you will," he said.

"I don't know what you're talking about. I'll remember what?" Donovan turned to look at Joe, and noticed something in the other man's face. Something about his eyes. There was something in them, something in the pupils, like a shadow of something hiding in the black darkness of his pupils.

"Everything. You'll remember everything, General."

"I can't even remember what happened in the casino."

"Just like you can't move things with your mind?" Joe asked, and cracked a wry smile.

"What makes you think I can remember *everything*?"

"Because," Joe patted Donovan on the back again. "You're the one that made yourself forget."

The conference room at the Las Vegas Police Department was a zoo, complete with reporters, internal investigators and even a State Representative, who couldn't pass up a photo op, crowding the room as Bradley took the podium. He rustled some papers and files to make it look like he was gathering notes, and also to stall, then cleared his throat louder than normal to get everyone's attention.

"Thank you for coming, please everyone settle down and we can get this underway," Bradley rumbled. He waited a moment for the room to reach relative calm before continuing. "As you all know we have a fugitive on the loose in the area," Bradley clicked a button on a remote and the picture of Donovan came up on a screen behind him.

"Lieutenant, how confident is the LVPD that this man will be captured in a timely manner?" One of the reporters blurted out.

"Please, hold your questions to the end, thank you. This man, known as Donovan O'Connell, escaped custody last night after detonating some type of weapon, we're not sure what yet, in a casino showroom. He seemed to use a similar weapon to escape our facility here. How he smuggled it in, we're still looking into but it could have been in a, uh, unpleasant location," Bradley cleared his throat.

"We are working closely with the FBI and Homeland Security, and as this is an ongoing investigation I'm not able to divulge many other details, so please speak with our press liaison for all your questions, thank you." Bradley scooped up the files and made to leave the podium when the State Representative, a large man whose suit jacket barely contained the size of his stomach, stood up and spoke in a loud voice.

"Now wait one minute," he said, prompting Bradley to stop and turn to face the crowd once more. "It is my job as representative of this district to see that my constituents are safe, number one, and well informed about potential dangers, number two. Surely you can tell these good people of the press *something* more than 'the investigation is ongoing'? Don't you think these voters deserve more than that?"

Cameras clicked, lights swiveled to face Bradley again, and all eyes fell upon him. He stood there for a full fifteen seconds saying nothing, but counting the beats in his head before he would give an answer. Finally, it came.

"No." And with that, he left the podium, and the conference room, among a loud uproar of questions and comments alike.

Bradley took the long way back to his office, since the more immediate route was a crime scene with a gaping hole in the exterior wall of the third floor. As he neared his office, several of the officers in the bullpen looked his way, a few offering quick, conspicuous looks as though they were trying to warn him of something. He didn't pay much attention and opened the door to his office, then froze. Sitting opposite his desk was Security Agent Parker, and Special Agent Miller, but behind his desk, with back turned, was someone in his chair.

"Who the hell are you?" Bradley boomed. The chair spun around to face him, and in it sat a red-haired woman in a pencil skirt, white blouse and jacket. Her black heels had bright red soles, and she blinked rapidly and grinned as Bradley stood dumbfounded.

"There he is at last, the man of the hour," the woman said. "Please come in, Lieutenant, we've all been waiting for you."

Bradley closed the door behind him, shot the other two men quick glances but they didn't bother looking up at him.

"Lady, this morning has been one hell of a week, so you better spit it out and fast," Bradley said. The woman stood from the chair and stuck out her hand, but when Bradley didn't shake it, she simply held it there insistently.

"Meredith Brown. I'm part of a task force under the USMC Criminal Investigation Division, and I'll be needing any information you have concerning Donovan O'Connell right away," Meredith smiled, her hand turning from that of a handshake position to a palm up position.

"Well, Ms. Brown, we don't have jack on this guy," Bradley said, tossing the papers in his hand past her and onto his desk, then turning to a cabinet and pulling open a drawer. "When we tried to I.D. him last night, everything came up flagged as fake," Bradley removed three glasses, then looked over his shoulder at Meredith, who raised an eyebrow. Bradley pulled out a fourth glass.

"I called these boys to come and take a look and to my knowledge they didn't find anything since last night," both agents shook their heads, so Bradley poured from a whiskey bottle and offered them each a glass. "I didn't see the remodel of our station with my own eyes, I was a bit behind having been stuck behind a desk. Literally." Bradley poured two more, corked the bottle and offered a glass to Meredith. They toasted and he took a swig.

"So," Bradley continued, "what can you tell *us* that might shed some light on this very odd situation we find ourselves in?" Meredith sipped her whiskey and smiled.

"Not a single thing. My department will be taking over this investigation," she cooed.

"Uh, excuse me, ma'am, but no you will not," Agent Parker chimed in. "Homeland Security has jurisdiction in this case." Special Agent Miller cleared his throat, loudly, so Parker added, "we're working in close ties with the FBI. If you'd like to be briefed on our findings we can arrange that."

Meredith raised her eyebrows and set down her glass, then sat on the edge the desk and crossed her arms over her chest. "Well well, it sounds like you have it all taken care of, Security Agent Parker," she said with a wry smile. "Tell me, what *do* you know about Mr. O'Connell?"

"We are, uh, putting together that information, uh at the moment and as soon as we have it I can relay that to you," Parker said. "Once I clear your actual jurisdiction with your superiors," he added.

"My superiors? I see," Meredith turned and grabbed her glass, downing the contents, then placed it gingerly on the desk again. "In that case, you'll need to call the White House," she winked then looked at Bradley. "I'll expect everything you *do* have, including evidence from the showroom in my office. Which will be…here," she said holding her hands out.

"Excuse me?" Bradley asked, his voice lowering even more than usual.

"Until we get this mess cleaned up, you and I Lieutenant are going to be roommates. I'll be the Ying to your

Yang, so the sooner I get answers and we find your fugitive, the sooner I get my happy ass back to Washington. Got it?"

"I assume I don't have much choice in the matter," Bradley said, a statement more than a question.

"You are a smart boy. Now, tell me everything about last night. Where you picked up our John, what his mental state was, did he say anything, anything peculiar you witnessed…" Meredith started.

"You mean like how he pinned us three grown men to a wall with a metal table?" Agent Miller chimed in.

"That's a good start," Meredith reached into her purse and pulled out a small tablet and a stylus, then immediately began jotting things down.

"Yes, a table that was bolted to the concrete floor," Bradley added. "Or how he was able to blow an eight foot hole in a sixteen inch thick wall made of concrete and steel. I've never seen that, and I've been to a lot of magic shows in my day."

"Let's just say our John is not your average magician," Meredith said without looking up. "What else?"

"What exactly *is* your John, then?" Bradley pressed, as he finished his whiskey. Meredith merely smiled to her tablet.

"What else?" She said, ignoring the question.

"Homeland has labeled this guy a domestic terrorist," Agent Parker said, "and we believe he's using some kind of experimental weapon of mass destruction."

"Is that the best you've got?" Meredith asked, this time looking Parker directly in the eyes.

"Yes, ma'am, that's as far as we've gotten before we analyze the debris at the crime scene."

"And when will that be?"

"We have agents collecting and processing items right now, but it's a delicate process what with the level of destruction, plus injuries and loss of human life," Parker trailed off.

"All right, Miller, what does the FBI know?" Meredith asked, as she grabbed her whiskey glass and held it up to Bradly, who took it begrudgingly.

"We're in the process of going through his last four years of transactions, bank history, etcetera. Basically this guy is a ghost before three and a half years ago. Whoever did his forgeries is an artist because they even got by our databases when he purchased a gun about a year ago."

"I'm not surprised, but that is impressive, thank you Bradley," Meredith took the glass from Bradley and had another sip.

"Why doesn't that surprise you?" Bradley asked. "Or do I already know the answer?"

"Do you?" Meredith asked, looking up at him.

"It doesn't surprise you because he's one of yours," Bradley said. "Your people did the forgeries and got him into the system."

Meredith pursed her lips. "Ooo, close, but no. He's that good because he *was* one of ours, yes. But we didn't get him into the system, he did that on his own."

"Why are we spinning our wheels when you could find him without us? What's the point in us even being here?" Parker asked, getting annoyed.

"Okay, this is going to take forever, and we don't have forever," Meredith put her tablet down and looked all three men over for a moment. "Fine, you know what I'll read you in. It's obvious none of you know anything helpful, but I *do* need your help in finding this guy. Yes, he was one of ours, he went A.W.O.L. four years ago. But you're sniffing down the wrong goose here. He doesn't possess a weapon of mass destruction."

"Then what in the world does he have than can do that kind of damage?" Bradley insisted.

"Lieutenant, this man *is* a weapon of mass destruction," Meredith said, as she downed her whiskey and picked her tablet back up. "So I suggest you use every available resource you have to find him, before he does a repeat of last night. Or much, much worse."

Chapter 4
The General and the Simpleton

"Hey honey, it's me, again. Look I don't know what happened back at the show, but I really need to know that you're safe. I know these calls are from weird numbers but, please, please pick up. I love you." Donovan closed the flip phone and tossed it on the kitchen counter while Joe looked through a collection of hats on the table.

"She won't pick up," Joe muttered.

"Of course she won't if you keep making me call with burner phones. She has no idea whose calling," Donovan shot back.

"Your phone is gone."

"I know that. But I just," Donovan sighed and rubbed his hands through his hair. "I need to know that she's okay."

"You should be doing the thing. You could be g-g-getting better," Joe said. Donovan held out a hand and a hat flipped through the air from the table into his hands. He immediately winced as a searing pain shot down the back of his skull. Joe turned and lit up, delighted.

"You did it!" He shouted.

"Yeah, yeah I'm a circus clown. I can move hats. Big deal. I just want my normal life back." Donovan rubbed the back of his head and tilted it left and right, popping his neck.

"What normal life?" Joe stood from the table and moved to a cabinet under the sink. He stooped down and opened it, and pulled out a cardboard box that had seen better days and was covered in dust. He blew on the box, sending dust in all directions and set it down on the table.

"What's that?" Donovan asked, moving to meet Joe at the table.

"You were a big Ge-gen-general. You worked on a big project. That's how we met," Joe opened the box and turned it upside down, dumping dozens of files and paper all over the table.

"What are you talking about?" Donovan picked up a file and opened it, seeing heavily redacted documents inside. "What is all this?"

"You don't remember. You had to forget so you wouldn't remember," Joe started sorting through the files more haphazardly, looking for something specific.

"I don't remember what? What do you actually know about me?" Donovan picked up another file, finding it filled with the same type of papers, all mostly blacked out with no real information on them. "How did you get all this?" He paused when he came across a photo of himself, dressed in Marine Corp fatigues.

"See? I told you. Big General," Joe said, still sifting through various papers.

"I don't remember this. I never served in the military. This has to be fake," Donovan shook his head and tossed the photo down onto another paper. Then he paused and noticed the logo on the letterhead of one of the documents. He picked it up slowly and focused on the logo at the letterhead. It was an eye in the middle of a rifle crosshair, like that in a rifle scope.

"What is this? Do you recognize this?" Donovan held up the paper to Joe, who gasped and snatched it out of Donovan's hand.

"Here it is! See?! This is the project. You ran this project!" He handed the document back to Donovan, who studied it closely for a minute.

"There's nothing on here explaining what it is. Just more redacted stuff and some general information but nothing really solid. What is this logo? I've seen this logo before."

"Esp it," Joe smiled and shrugged. Donovan raised an eyebrow.

"Do what now?"

E...s...p! You can see wa-what isn't there!" Joe said smiling.

"Joe, that's not real. That was all debunked in the nineties. E.S.P. is just some carnival trick."

"Like moving things with T.K.?" Joe smiled broadly.

"I..." Donovan hung his head a moment and looked back up in frustration. "I don't know how to do what you're asking. This is getting me nowhere!" Donovan stood and slammed his fist on the table, directly on the document.

Suddenly he jerked, and his eyes rolled back in his head, as his fist was locked unmoving on the document. The logo of the eye with crosshairs in the middle swirled around in his brain, and just then he saw it everywhere.

On the wall.

On a door.

On a coffee mug.

On hundreds of papers that flitted around the room like they had been blown by an invisible fan.

Donovan tensed, unable to move, unable to breathe, seeing images in the back of his mind as his body randomly twitched and convulsed. Then he was in the desert. Mountains in the far distance but flat as far as the eye could see. There was a concrete dome, small, no larger than a shack, with a rusted steel door.

In an instant he was at the door, and he reached for it with his free hand, but it was locked and likely rusted shut. But then he saw it, a small metal plate on the steel doorframe that was slightly bent, as though something had struck it and misshapen it. But on the small plate, was the logo.

Donovan snapped back and gasped in deep, drawing in a great gulp of air and nearly collapsed on the floor. He caught himself with his free hand on the table as his knees gave out. He heaved to catch his breath and blinked rapidly, as though his eyes had been held open for hours and were completely dry, and now drew fresh tears to replenish them. His head felt like it was about to split open, so he grabbed at the top with both hands, desperate to keep from exploding.

"What… the hell… was that?!" He said with some effort as he looked over at Joe.

"You esp'd," Joe said matter of factly. "You saw it d-d-didn't you? You saw the place. The place in the desert somewhere. I saw it a long time ago, but I can't s-s-see it anymore."

"*That* was… the E.S.P. thing!? That was terrible! I couldn't move! I could hardly breathe! Oh God, my head!" Donovan sat down slowly to keep from passing out.

"That w-was your specialty. You could see anything anywhere. That's why you're the General," Joe said and looked down at his feet. "You could do everything. Not like me."

"The desert. I saw a desert. And papers, and a coffee mug? Everything had that logo on it, though. Everything. Like a company or a business or something. Agh my head… does it always do this?"

Joe slowly shook his head, then answered.

Page 40

"Or a project," he offered. "Military project."

"Look I don't know what's happening to me, and I can't get ahold of my wife or check hospitals to see if she's okay but..." Donovan froze a moment and made eye contact with Joe. "I have got to figure out what the hell is going on. If you've got answers, I'm willing to listen." His breathing slowly returned to normal as the pain in his head subsided.

One of the burner cell phones suddenly rang, and Donovan nearly fell over as he thrust himself at the table to grab it and lift it to his cheek.

"Hello? Kathy? Did you get my message?"

"You did what I told you," a man's voice came on the other end, "and you're still alive. Good."

"You," Donovan whispered. "Who are you? I want answers."

"Don't worry, General, you'll get your answers. Tell me what you found and I can help you."

"I'm here in some... house. With a guy named Joe. He says he knows me, he has files and a picture of me and..." Donovan trailed off.

"Joe, huh? Interesting," the man said. "Stay with him, do what he says. I'll be in touch with more information shortly."

"Wait!" Donovan shouted. "My wife, Kathy, do you know anything about my wife?"

"Don't worry about Kathy, Mr. O'Connell. I'll look into it for you. You just stick close to Joe, I'll be in touch."

The line went dead. Donovan set the phone down slowly then turned his eyes to Joe. He looked at Donovan and shook his head solemnly. "We have to go. They'll find my t-tr-truck," Joe said, pointing to the muted TV, where reports were showing roadblocks being established through the state.

"Where can we possibly go? I don't have any contacts that would let me couch surf, much less you," Donovan said. Joe smiled and held up the document with the logo on the letterhead.

"We'll go find this. Maybe they can help you find answers. Might know about your wife, too," Joe shrugged.

Donovan considered the words of the mysterious man on the phone. He had been right about the truck waiting for him outside the police station, maybe it was worth a shot listening to Joe now. "You really think that's the way to go?"

"They had a picture of you. They might know wuh-why you have so many specialities," Joe grinned. It was flimsy reasoning, and it detracted from his search for his wife, but it was possible they might find some answers.

"Fine, but where do we look?" Donovan asked. Joe smiled and tapped Donovan on the forehead.

"You know. The desert."

The Las Vegas Police Department was a flurry of activity, now that Meredith was running the operation. Everything except for extreme emergencies, like homicides, was put on the back burner. Even calls from the local hotels and casinos were going unanswered, leaving them to fend for themselves. Most the police force felt the casinos would rather prefer to mete out their own justice anyway.

Meredith had quickly established roadblocks at every major exit to the entire county, hoping that would turn up something at the very least. The police put out an all-points bulletin for the truck that Donovan was spotted climbing into, though they couldn't identify the driver of the truck with nothing but the low light, heavily pixelated image from the security cameras. Still it was a start.

"Did you find him? Where is he?" Meredith demanded of one of the officers as she marched down the hall.

"He's waiting for you in interrogation. Uh…"

"Yes? Hurry up and spit it out," Meredith huffed.

"He's really shaken up, ma'am. He might not be too much help," the officer said, as he opened the door for Meredith. She disregarded him and headed into the interrogation room, her entire demeanor shifting.

"Hi, thank you so much for coming. I know this is a huge inconvenience for you," she said, as she held out a hand. The hypnotist Marc Julien extended a shaky hand and shook hers like a limp noodle, then retracted and crossed his arms over his chest.

"No, no it's all right," he murmured.

"So, first of all, Mr. Julien—"

"It's actually Rosenberg. Matthew Rosenberg. Marc Julien is just my stage name," Matthew said. Then he added, "No one would come see 'The Great Rosenberg'."

"Ok then, Mr. Rosenberg. I want you to understand you are not in any sort of trouble. We just need some information from you, that's all," Meredith said, using her best comforting and consoling voice. Matthew scoffed but nodded. Suddenly the door opened and Bradley's imposing frame filled the doorway. He stepped inside as an officer closed and locked the door behind him, then he dragged a chair from the corner of the room to the table, shot Meredith a look, and sat down.

"Mr. Rosenberg," Meredith began, "this is Lieutenant Bradley."

"Uh huh, we've met," Bradley snorted, drawing a quizzical look from Meredith.

"Is that so?" She asked.

"The 'Mentalist' here took one thousand dollars from my daughter to help her quit smoking. After a nervous breakdown she now smokes a pack a day," Bradley said, staring Matthew down, who wouldn't make eye contact.

"Please understand," Matthew said, barely above a whisper.

"Speak up, boy," Bradley growled.

"Please understand," Matthew cleared his throat and started over, "that what I do is simply offer suggestions. The mind will do what it wants. People can only be hypnotized if they *want* to be. Obviously your daughter didn't…" Matthew stopped himself short before going any further, as Bradley leaned forward, his chair groaning to match the growl in his belly.

"Go ahead, finish that sentence," he said, glaring at Matthew who sat back and shook his head.

"I think the real reason we have asked you to come here today, Mr. Rosenberg," Meredith smiled, shot Bradley a look of warning, and smiled again at Matthew, "is to get your statement on what happened two nights ago at your show." Matthew nodded, crossed his legs, and began chewing on his thumbnail.

"Go on, *Mr.* Rosenberg. Tells us what you saw," Bradley said, as he leaned back in his own chair.

"Like I said," Matthew began again, "I only give suggestions. I don't actually do anything to the participants. I've seen it a hundred times… someone will come up on stage, I do my bit, and they just chuckle or make faces at the audience mocking me. It's humiliating, but it is what it is. Not everyone *will* be hypnotized. Only those that want to be."

"Did Mr. O'Connell want to be?" Meredith asked. Matthew chewed his nail harder.

"That man, he was perfectly nice. Looked like a normal mark..." Matthew looked up and saw both cops looking back with blank expressions. "A mark, someone that's easy to spot and easy to manipulate. He looked like an easy mark to get the show started. He was willing to come up and give it a try, but..." Matthew trailed off.

"But what?" Bradley asked.

"But there was something else about him. The moment he closed his eyes... the moment I started guiding him into a relaxed state... I don't know, no, I don't *think* anyone else could have seen it from the audience, but I did. I watched his face, his cheeks, his mouth, everything... change."

Meredith drew in a long breath, and caught Bradley looking at her in the corner of her eye. She didn't make eye contact with him.

"Go on, please, if you can," she encouraged. Matthew nodded, and took a breath as well.

"As the subject relaxes, there needs to be a catalyst to shock them into a suggestible state. A noise, a clap, a thump on the chest. I use a snap," Matthew stopped chewing his nail and looked down at the table. "I snapped my fingers, and his eyes shot open...and they..."

"They what?" Meredith insisted.

"Black," Matthew said, his eyes growing wider. "They were black."

"What do you mean? They changed color from green or what?" Bradley leaned forward, less intimidating and more intrigued. Matthew shook his head quickly.

"No, I mean everything. Pupil, iris, everything. There wasn't any white or veins or anything. They were completely black. Like a shark," Matthew was trembling, and had returned to chewing on his nails. His leg jumped up and down on the ball of his foot and he stared at the table.

"What happened next, Mr. Rosenberg?" Meredith asked in a calm, soothing tone.

"He pushed me with one hand. One. And I flew backwards on the stage, and then my jacket was just... on fire."

"He lit your jacket on fire?" Bradley asked.

"Hush please," Meredith snapped. "Go on."

"I took my jacket off and he was standing... no... *floating* on the edge of the stage waving his arms, left right left right, one after another. And I saw chairs and tables and... and *people* just flying through the air! And he was grinning this terrifying grin and just laughing and people were screaming and..." Matthew suddenly put both hands over his ears and leaned forward, his face inches from the table.

"I can still hear them screaming..." he whispered.

Meredith calmly produced a small hand purse, opened it up and removed a syringe. She pulled off the protective tip from the needle and stabbed it into Matthew's shoulder. In a moment, Matthew's forehead rested on the table, and he was completely unconscious. She put the syringe back in her bag, and looked at an incredulous Bradley.

"What did you just do?" He demanded.

"I put him to sleep, obviously."

"But why?"

"Didn't you see how nervous he was? He'll wake up and feel like a million dollars. Besides, we got what we needed from him," Meredith said, then stood and went to leave the room until Bradley grabbed her wrist and stood himself.

"Just wait one minute. Do you believe anything that boy just said? Chairs flying through the air with a wave of his hand? Eyes as black as a shark's? C'mon now, I didn't take you for a lunatic."

"Release my wrist or I'll break yours in five places," Meredith snapped. Bradley made a face and let her go. "And for your information, yes, I believe everything that boy just told us, because I have good *reason* to believe it."

"Here's the part where you let me in on the big government secret, or get out of my town," Bradley said, with a low growl. Meredith looked up at the surveillance camera and drew her hand across her throat. A moment later the red recording light stopped blinking.

"All right, Lieutenant. I'll do you this one favor, and don't say I never did anything for you. Our government on any given day is running a number of programs you've never heard of and never will. The goal of these programs is to create a better, safer, more sustainable world for your children and grandchildren," Meredith spoke very slowly as she looked Bradley directly in the eyes.

"You're talking about black sites. Off the books, secret codenames, not entirely legal, all that bull," Bradley said.

"The very same. Ninety-nine percent of them are complete duds, a waste of time and resources, but every now and then we hit the jackpot. But the reward is not always worth the effort, I'm afraid."

"Let me guess, Donovan O'Connell is one of those jackpots? And you released him out into my city."

"Released? Oh no. O'Connell was a jackpot, true, but we didn't release him anywhere. He broke out. And if you think what he did to your precinct was bad, you haven't seen him at his full potential."

"Then why don't you track him down and hit him with a warhead or something?" Bradley shook his head.

"I already told you, Lieutenant. He *is* the warhead. We are dealing with a weapon so highly advanced he is nothing like anything the world has seen. And the last thing we want is for him to come into his full potential again."

"Ok, next question. Why are you bothering me with this? Shouldn't the whole government be looking for this man if he is that dangerous?"

"He was part of a program Congress never approved, and the President didn't sign off on," Meredith said, her voice beginning to tremble. "And almost everyone else ever involved in it, is either also missing, or dead. We had hoped he had died, since he was off the grid for years. But now it seems all our worst fears have come back to haunt us. Those of us that are left anyway."

Bradley pinched the bridge of his nose and shook his head, then eyed Meredith. "How many are left?"

"Including me and O'Connell? Five. And two of them are just lab geeks that were reassigned years ago."

"And the other one?"

"In the wind. Like O'Connell was, until now. But the other one is about as harmless as you are, Lieutenant."

Bradley raised an eyebrow.

"What happens if we don't find O'Connell soon?" Bradley asked. "What happens if he... reaches his full potential?"

"There will be hell to pay."

———————————

The old pickup truck sped along Interstate 40 with Donovan behind the wheel and Joe in the passenger seat. He had a large roadmap spread out over the dashboard, and kept encroaching on Donovan's space as he drew a finger along the map on various places. Donovan did his best to ignore his traveling companion, feeling the simple man might be his best bet at figuring out what was happening to him.

They had decided to leave Las Vegas and follow the only clue they really had. The desert from Donovan's vision. He had seen a very flat barren space with mountain ranges on both sides. Joe had deduced that the best possible location that might fit the bill, would be White Sands, New Mexico.

"Here," Joe shouted suddenly, startling Donovan and thrusting his finger onto a point on the map. "Look here."

"I'm driving, can't you just tell me what it is?" Donovan replied angrily.

"Right by White Sands. Holloman Air Force Base."

"Ok, what about it?"

"Maybe that's where you made you forget," Joe pulled the map back and stared at it intently.

"Or," Donovan shook his head, "there's an air force base there because White Sands is where they test missiles and bombs and have for years. Not some secret government base, it's all pretty well documented."

"But the logo. W-wh-what is the logo then?" Joe shot back at Donovan. Truly he didn't have an answer, and secretly wanted to know why there was a photo of him in a Marine uniform among the papers Joe had.

"This is all kind of ridiculous I hope you know," Donovan said, trying to change the topic. "Driving across the country with a stranger I've never met, in a truck that's probably stolen, planning to what, knock on the door of a military installation and hope they let us in? I have really got to be out of my mind."

"I'm not a stranger. You know me. You tr-tr-trained me. Maybe they will recognize you and your rank and let us in. Then someone can fix you," Joe said.

"Fix me? I'm moving things with my mind and seeing places I've never been, and someone is going to fix that? Well I hope so, because this... this is not living. I just want my regular life back."

Joe regarded Donovan for a few minutes, and just stared at him while he drove until Donovan started to become agitated and nervous by it.

"What? Why are you just staring at me like that?"

"I feel s-s-sad for you."

"Why?"

"Because you don't remember how powerful and cool you were. You were really great and now you don't remember that. That's sad to me."

"Yeah well I hate to break it to you, pal, but whatever you think you remember about me isn't true. I'm not some psychic soldier and I never served in the Marines," Donovan looked over at Joe awkwardly. "I respect people that serve. It just... it wasn't me."

"Just wait," Joe smiled, as he laid his seat back and pulled his ball cap over his eyes. "You'll see."

Donovan cracked his neck and glanced over only once to see Joe was snoring within minutes of closing his eyes, leaving Donovan alone to his thoughts as he drove across Northern Arizona. High above a helicopter passed by, and though it was quite a distance, and the windows were rolled up, Donovan could swear he could hear the sound of the rotors thumping through the air.

It was a pleasant, almost relaxing sound to him. It echoed in his mind as he stared at the road before him, keeping a safe distance from other cars and letting those that wanted by to pass around him. The helicopter was all he could think about, though, even as the mountains of Flagstaff drew nearer and nearer, and the actual helicopter was long since gone.

The thumping blades resounded in his mind.

He had been on one, not too long ago, soaring over land and lakes and mountains. Even with the headset on he could still hear the rotors and it was always a pleasant sound to him, no matter where he was. The helicopter touched down and Donovan replaced the headphones with his hat, as he and another Marine… maybe a woman… ran from the chopper as it lifted off into the sky again.

The other Marine, yes definitely a woman, held out a hand and led Donovan from the helipad to a concrete dome with a rusted red door. She swiped a card and entered a few digits, and the door opened. She held it for him and he removed his hat and entered, the woman following close behind. The door closed and there was a strange whirring sound.

Donovan blinked and swerved the truck as another car tried to merge onto the highway in front of him without either speeding up and slowing down. Both vehicles swerved and tried to correct themselves, but the car overcorrected and soon was fishtailing wildly across both lanes in front of Donovan. He hit his brakes just as the other car swung by, nearly missing their front end. Then the worst happened.

The car, still moving forward, turned too sharply and ended up perpendicular to the flow of traffic. The front passenger tire blew out, and the momentum was just enough for the car to flip. The car rolled across the highway twice and ended up completely upside down, traffic coming to a stand still behind Donovan and Joe.

"What happened?" Joe asked, sitting up and pulling his hat on straight. "Uh oh."

Donovan sat frozen behind the wheel, his heart racing after narrowly missing the other car.

"Oh my gosh. What do we do? We can't... we can't just sit here. The cops will want to see my ID and know I've escaped jail. What do we do?" Donovan asked in a panic.

"We need to move the car," Joe shrugged. "You can. It's your specialty."

"Will you stop saying that?! I could barely turn the television on. There's no way I can move a car! Come on, we have to push! We have to push it and save the passengers. Hurry!"

Donovan put the truck in park, pried his white-knuckled fingers off the wheel, and leapt from the truck. He ran to the overturned car and squatted down next to the window to look inside.

"Are you okay? Is anyone hurt?" He ask frantically. There was a man and a women in the front seat, both hanging upside down and both seemingly uninjured, at first sight. "I'm going to get you out of there!"

Donovan looked around for a pole, a branch, something to use as a lever, but nothing was just lying around on the highway. He pressed his back against the car and gripped the door and tried to lift the car to right it again, but unsurprisingly it didn't budge.

"Come on, General. You can do it. You h-have to," Joe said, as he lumbered over to where Donovan stood.

"You grab that end and I'll grab the door and maybe we..." Joe waved him, off.

"Do the thing. The whoosh thing. TK," Joe said, pointing to the car. "Look. P-p-people are getting out of their cars. They'll recognize you."

"Damnit!" Donovan shouted. He placed his hands against the door as though he was going to push. Suddenly the car groaned and the side window shattered, but the car began slowly rolling right side up again. "Augh!" Donovan screamed as his head began to pound.

He could hear his heartbeat.

His vision blurred.

Not this time. Have to. Move it.

He could feel the car, not just the metal of the door, but the paint, the gears that raised the window, the door latch and it's components. He could *feel* the car. He pulled his hands off the metal and turned to face the car, hands outstretched.

"Do it. Do it," Joe chanted.

"Just… give me a hand here… please…" Donovan grunted, and the car slowly began to roll onto it's side.

"C'mon… you… stupid…" Donovan strained as the pain began to grow from the back of his skull, making sweat run down his forehead. But the car kept righting itself. With a loud creak and crash the car fell back onto it's three good tires. Heaving for breath, he set his foot on the back tire to keep balance.

"Gotta m-m-move it," Joe muttered. Donovan looked over his shoulder to see the car was still perpendicular with the road, and blocking any flow of traffic. He'd have to spin the car around if he wanted to flee the scene.

Suddenly Joe placed his foot against the same tire Donovan rested on and gave it a hard push. The car spun ninety degrees like a bulldozer had hit it. Donovan looked up at Joe who merely grinned back.

Joe patted him on the back and smiled. "You good? We have to go now," he said. Donovan clenched his teeth, desperately willing the searing pain in his skull to subside. He nodded at Joe and staggered back to the truck.

"The cops are going to find us now. No way we can avoid them after what just happened," he said in a panic.

"Nah, they'll be too busy cleaning up the mess. We'll be g-g-gone by the time they start to look for us," Joe said, as he pulled his cap over his eyes again.

"Fleeing the scene of an accident. That's a crime. Another crime I'm adding to my list lately." Donovan put the truck into gear and peeled the tires out as they roared past the confused older couple and sped down the interstate. His vision returned and the headache left once more.

"You'll add more to that list, don't worry," Joe said.

"There's something else," Donovan glanced at Joe who was already snoring. "Yeah, thanks for helping back there. Oh wait, you just let me do it all." He shook his head and turned his eyes back to the wide open road.

Chapter 5
Whispers

Bradley sat in his office poring over images and reports and evidence from the incident at the casino. It was still very surreal to him to even think that the government had been successful in creating some kind of psychic, super soldier. Even more surreal was the fact that such a person had been roaming around in his city for almost four years and went completely unnoticed. Or the fact that the government *lost* someone of this caliber and hadn't put forth effort to find him. No, that wasn't surreal, that was just plain ridiculous.

He had been on the force for thirty-two years now, and during that time he had seen some very strange things in the city of Las Vegas. Even when pushed to retire after his twenty-five year mark, Bradley stayed on and kept working, he liked it. He had grown accustomed to the occasional outlandish event, like stage tigers attacking their trainer, or a magic show gone wrong, or even a sniper opening fire on a crowded concert.

But one thing he had never seen before was the chaos that took place at the Atlantis Hotel and Casino. He wouldn't have believed it if he hadn't seen the destruction with his own eyes, and even then it was hard to believe what had actually caused it. Bradley was still holding to the bomb theory, except after hearing the testimony from the hypnotist, the supernatural was seeming more and more likely. Then there was the attack inside his own precinct, which he got to see first hand again, as O'Connell pinned him and two other fully grown men to a wall with a metal table. All of it was just so uncanny that it just couldn't be fake.

Bradley found himself staring at his computer screen, eyes glazed over with his mind deep in thought when Special Agent Miller opened the door and knocked.

"You need to see this," Miller said, then disappeared back out of the door. Bradley stood up with a groan, it had been a long few days and he figured things were only going to get worse from here. He walked down the hall to a conference room that had been set up as a war room for the current operation, which was to find and stop Donovan O'Connell.

Bradley stepped into the busy room and immediately made eye contact with Meredith, who strode over to him with a sense of purpose.

"We've got an incident just outside Flagstaff, Arizona. A car accident involving an old pickup truck and another vehicle. The second vehicle apparently rolled and ended up on its own roof, when witnesses say a man came out of the pickup, grabbed the other car, and flipped it right side up, single handedly," Meredith raised an eyebrow. "Sound wild? It just might be our guy."

"Did anyone get an ID on the guy? Do we know where he was headed?" Bradley asked.

"Witnesses say he got back in the truck and took off, headed East," Meredith held up a printed picture from a traffic camera. Bradley studied it a moment and shook his head.

"This doesn't show us anything. It's a blurry image of a person on the road and a truck. And another car right side up, but other than that I can't make out if it's our boy or not."

"Of course it is," Meredith said. "I've got satellites searching Interstate 40 for that truck. The moment we get a ping we'll lock on and find out where he's headed."

"It's flimsy," Bradley said with a shake of his head. "Plus if he's in Arizona now, that's outside my jurisdiction. I can't do anything except request extradition when and if he's picked up by one of their boys."

"You may not have jurisdiction, but I do. And so do your two men from the FBI and Homeland," Meredith said, as she tucked the papers into a folder.

"Great, let me know when you find him," Bradley said and turned to walk away.

"You're giving up just like that?" Meredith called after him. He paused and sighed and turned around to face her again.

"What do you want me to do? Huh? I have no legal authority to cross state lines and pursue this guy. And if he's headed East he won't be in Arizona for long. Soon it'll be New Mexico's problem to grab him. Maybe we can give them a heads-up and nab him at the border." Bradley rubbed his forehead and sighed again. "I don't have the manpower, or the resources to go on a nationwide manhunt, even if I could."

Meredith walked over to him casually and set the file down on a table. She reached out and took Bradley's tie, fixing it for him as she spoke softly.

"I need to bring O'Connell in. But I can't do it alone, and I need to do it without too much of a mess. Messes result in investigations, which result in committees, which results in my ass jumping from courtroom to courtroom for two years telling people that they aren't cleared to receive a classified briefing. I would very much like your help," Meredith said, even quieter than before.

"Ms. Brown…"

"Have your Fed deputize you and let's get on the road. We can catch him, even if we need to fly over his head. The one thing we don't want is for him to get wherever he's going," Meredith smiled but swallowed hard.

"There's more you're not telling me," Bradley said.

"A lot more. Suffice it to say, it's best for everyone to catch O'Connell and neutralize him as quickly as possible. I think you and I are in agreement on that."

Bradley nodded slowly, then looked over to the conference table in the war room.

"Hey Miller, come here a minute," Bradley said as he stepped away. Meredith smiled and checked her watch. She glanced back at Bradley and quickly slipped out of the room.

"Do you have eyes on target yet," Meredith said quietly into her phone from the ladies' room.

"In position, awaiting your orders," the hushed voice on the other end replied.

"We've spotted him on I-40 heading East, but there's no guarantee he'll keep to the highway, especially after that accident."

"You're sure it's him?" The voice asked.

"Who else can single-handedly lift a car? Maybe you. Yeah it's him," Meredith said.

"Good. I'll pick him off at Gallup after you confirm he crosses the border. You better be right about this," the voice said, hesitation in his voice.

"Just do your job. We get one shot then we lose the element of surprise. You and I both know we can't take him otherwise. I'll be in contact." Meredith ended the call, then quickly washed her hands and headed out of the bathroom and towards the conference room.

"Well? Are you with me or not?" She asked as she walked up to Bradley and Miller. Miller gave her a quick glance then turned and strode off quickly. "What's his problem?

"He's got to take it up the chain before he can authorize me on this little field trip," Bradley said with a flash of a smile. "Why don't you go on ahead, and I'll keep running intelligence from here. If I find anything useful I'll let you know. Besides, you don't want me slowing you down."

Meredith stared directly into Bradley's eyes for a long moment, her face unmoving, like she was playing a game of poker with him and had a winning hand. Then Bradley noticed something different, something change in her eyes. It was almost as though streaks of red were crawling in and mixing with the green pigment of Meredith's irises. He tried not to stare but it was hard not to see it now that he had noticed it.

She blinked, and the red vanished.

"Suit yourself, Lieutenant," she said. "I'll let you know when we grab him." Meredith walked by, brushing shoulders with Bradley as she did, leaving him alone. He slowly looked down at the folded piece of paper Miller had slipped into his hand while they had spoke away from Meredith, and opened it with his forefinger and thumb. One look was all he needed before folding it back up and slipping it into his pocket.

"I need a coffee," he announced loudly to no one in particular, then exited the conference room and headed straight for the elevator.

"So you're like me, then?" Donovan asked, looking over to Joe briefly before returning his eyes to the road.

"Like you? No. You do lots of things. I only d-d-do one thing. I move things," Joe replied.

"Like me. I move things too, apparently."

"Big things. I move little things," Joe said and hung his head. "That car was a b-b-big thing. I watched you. You just… placed your hands on it and rolled it over like it was a wheel of cheese, not a two ton vehicle," Joe smiled. "It's your specialty," he added.

"Yeah, my specialty. I seem to have a lot of 'specialties' according to you. But I can't seem to figure out what they are or how to really use them," Donovan grunted.

"They'll make you remember," Joe pointed to the logo on a piece of paper that he still clung to.

"Okay, let's talk about that for a minute. I don't know where you think we're going, and what you think we're going to do when we get there. You know that *if* there's some kind of military or government installation there, there is no way in Hell they are going to just open the doors and welcome us in with open arms," Donovan said, his voice growing louder as he spoke.

"You're the General. They know you. We won't have any tr-trouble," Joe retorted.

"Let's just say, for the sake of argument, that you're right. We find this secret base and everyone rolls out the red carpet because I'm 'the General'. Except I have absolutely no memory whatsoever of any of this. I've been living my life with a good paying job, a loving wife, and a fantasy football team for years. So all of that was just fake?"

"Yes," Joe nodded. "You made you forget. They'll make you remember." Donovan pinched the bridge of his nose with one hand and sighed.

"It must be nice being so simple," he said, condescendingly. Joe slowly turned to look at Donovan, a look of both sadness and disgust on his face.

"No. You made me forget, too. I was smart. Now I'm n-n-not. You did this to me, too. It's not nice. You aren't nice," Joe growled, then turned back facing forward again.

"I... I did... what?" Donovan kept stealing glances at Joe but he was done talking, and so the two of them stayed in silence for serval miles.

True, he had had the worst forty-eight hours of his life, and things didn't look like they would be getting better for a while at least. But that didn't give him any right to belittle or abuse the one person who had been helpful thus far. At the very least he could show a little respect for the man.

Donovan reached over with his right hand and held it out in front of Joe.

"Look I... I apologize. That was rude of me. I shouldn't assume that you didn't also have a rough time at the hands of these... whoever they are. I'm sorry." Joe looked over at Donovan, then shook his hand, nearly crushing Donovan's hand in the process. Donovan winced in pain, and felt some odd tingle course down his arm to his hand, subtly peeling Joe's hand off his own.

Then he saw Joe in the mirror, standing behind himself. Joe stared blankly at him as he stared blankly into his own eyes. Outside the room there was someone barking orders, loud but indiscernible. Donovan looked from himself to Joe, who slowly nodded and rested a hand on his shoulder. Donovan's eyes lit up blue, but also yellow but also red but also not at all. He said something, like an incantation, but no words came out of his mouth.

The barking outside the room had turned into the barking of dogs, hundreds of them, rather than one man yelling orders at someone or some thing. Then the mirror in front of him rippled, like still water struck by a rock. It rippled and cracked into shards and shattered into a million pieces, and with it the wall it hung on, and the ceiling above and the floor below. Everything shattered and turned into grey dust. Everything except Donovan and Joe.

The two of them hung there in mid air, standing on some unseen floor as the floor beneath them became dust. Wood and concrete and glass and fire billowed all around them, but none of it touched Donovan or Joe, like a bubble had formed around them, protecting them. Everything suddenly sped up and the floor and ceiling, and half a building, fell down all around them, leaving them exposed in the sunlight.

Donovan turned his head to look, and in the distance dust was flying up as several Jeeps came charging towards he and Joe. The Jeeps stopped a few yards away and at least three stories down, as multiple faceless men and women stepped out of the vehicles and gazed up at them. Donovan looked down and saw one of the men wore jeans, a black blazer, and a white shirt with the profile and rifle crosshairs logo on it.

The faceless people began to cheer, their hands smashing together in a resounding echo that filled Donovan's ears and mind.

He released Joe's hand and looked forward, seeing a large green sign announcing that Holbrook was five miles away. He glanced at Joe who was staring back at him with a blank expression. Donovan cleared his throat, adjusted his seat, and refocused his eyes on the road.

"We'll turn South at Holbrook," he said. "We need to get off I-40. We'll take the 60 east instead," Donovan said to

Joe without looking over. Joe didn't say a word back, but turned his head and continued staring blankly out the windshield.

The FBI had produced two helicopters with the word "Police" written in bright blue letters on the both sides of the birds. Meredith immediately shot that idea down, and made a phone call. Within thirty minutes two Blackhawk helicopters were waiting for them at LVPD. Meredith and Agent Miller boarded one, and a few S.W.A.T. members boarded the other, then they were off and into the air.

No sooner did the birds clear the pad and take off into the sky, than Bradley marched down the hall towards the conference room and burst in like a bull.

"Parker! Where are you!?" He shouted, bringing the entire room to a stand still. Parker stood from a table, adjusted his tie, and calmly walked over to Bradley.

"Can I help you, Lieutenant?" He asked, somewhat quietly as the rest of the room went back to work.

"Care to explain this?" Bradley handed him the folded piece of paper he had received from Agent Miller. He unfolded it, read the words, and looked up shocked at Bradley.

"Who gave you this?" He asked.

"Our friend from the FBI. Agent Miller thought I should have it. You got something you want to tell me?"

"I have no idea what he means by this," Parker turned to walk away, but Bradley put a strong hand on his shoulder and stopped him.

"If that's the case, you won't have any problem with me calling Homeland to update them on the situation here, then would you?" Bradley said. Parker slowly turned, his entire demeanor turned dark as he looked at Bradley from under his eyebrows.

"If you want to keep that hand, I'd suggest you let me go, Lieutenant," he growled.

"I thought you might say that," Bradley nodded, staring directly into the other man's eyes. Parker blinked, and his eyes went from light brown, to black. Completely black, iris, pupil, everything. He gently reached up and took hold of Bradley's hand on his shoulder, and pried the fingers loose without any effort, causing Bradley to wince in pain.

Suddenly two other officers came up behind Parker, both grabbing an arm, while one stabbed a syringe into Parker's neck. He jumped in surprise, and started to throw the other officers off, but Bradley shot his free hand out like a snake and took hold of Parker's throat.

"Oh no you don't," he grunted, trying to help hold the man down. It was no use. Parker thrust a palm out into Bradley's chest, striking him hard enough to launch him backwards. He jerked the same arm back and struck one officer dead in the nose with his elbow. The officer's nose exploded like a strawberry, his head jerked back, and he slumped to the floor in a heap.

The second officer released Parker and jumped back in time to miss a wild swing that narrowly took out his jaw. Parker advanced on the man, backing him up against several desks as he scrambled for his life. A loud popping sound filled the room and Parker froze with gritted teeth as Bradley shot the man with his taser.

The taser ticked loudly every second but Parker managed to stay on his feet, though slowed incredibly. Another officer came out from behind a desk and fired her taser as well, the prongs sticking Parker in the neck.

Page 64

"*Gaahhh!*" He grunted at the pain of the prongs and the shock, but still his wild black eyes were fixed on the terrified officer pinned against the desks.

"Somebody grab him!" Bradley shouted. There was a hesitation from everyone in the room, then three more officers launched into action, all trying to tackle Parker to the ground. There was a sickening, blood curdling laugh from deep in Parker's throat, as he finally began to drop to the floor. His eyes returned to normal, and his body grew weak as the drugs began to take effect in Parker's bloodstream. At last his body became limp as he sank to the ground, face first, barely breathing.

Bradley stood up and panted for air as he hobbled over to the fallen officer.

"Are you all right, Lieutenant?" Someone asked. He nodded and pulled his shirt open, revealing a ballistic vest. He pulled a shattered ceramic plate from a front pouch and dropped it to the floor.

"Someone call the paramedics, right away! We've got a fallen officer," he huffed. "And get that, *thing to* a holding cell. I want his legs tied down and his arms bound around his chest. Use a straight jacket if we have one, I don't care. Until we get a handle on what the hell is happening here, I don't trust anyone from outside this precinct," Bradley announced.

The conference room burst into activity, but with a renewed purpose of scooping up and removing Agent Parker, while another officer took to phoning for an ambulance.

"The tracer you put on Agent Miller is active, sir," one officer said to Bradley. "We are monitoring them now and will know every move they make, so long as Miller is with them."

"Good. I need to know what that woman is really up to," Bradley said.

"Can I ask how you knew, sir?" The officer asked. Bradley picked up the folder piece of paper and handed it to her, as his attention fell to the downed officer in his arms.

CID: No record of Meredith Brown. Homeland: No current agent in the field/ LVPD.

Bradley sat down hard at his desk and breathed out a heavy sigh. He had no idea what was going on, what with a fake Homeland Security Agent, and a fake Criminal Investigations Division agent both in his station. Part of him wanted to just let the entire thing go and let the Feds handle this one. But what Agent Miller had said to him when he handed him the note, made him very, very uneasy.

"Someone is working very hard to cover this up," Miller had told him. "And they are very well connected."

He wanted to let it go, but the fact was that people had been injured, even killed in the attack at the Atlantis Hotel and Casino. One of his own officers was badly injured and wouldn't likely make it. Then there was that chilling testimony from the hypnotist he had heard. A man floating in mid air, with black eyes, causing untold destruction with a wave of his hand. He hadn't believed it, until just now when he saw "Agent" Parker's eyes turn black as well.

Bradley started to stand when his phone rang. He quickly scooped it up after the first ring and cleared his throat.

"This is Bradley," he barked.

"They are watching you," a man's voice said.

"Who is this? How'd you get this number?"

"Listen carefully, Lieutenant Bradley. Go to your liquor cabinet."

"No, you listen to me. I don't know what kind of a cop you think I am, but you think for one second—"

"We don't have time for games, Lieutenant. She put a camera in that cabinet," the man interrupted. "Believe me or not, she's watching you. Check for yourself."

The line suddenly disconnected.

Bradley put the phone down, while the vein in his forehead began to protrude. He took a deep breath and calmly walked over to the cabinet, opened it, and glanced around. Nothing seemed out of place.

"*Pshh*, prank calls." He began to close the cabinet doors and back away when the light reflected off something small that caught his eye. He paused, opened the door fully and leaned closer. There it was, no bigger than a pinky nail. The tiny lens of a tiny camera. A wire led out the back to the receiver the size of a Zippo lighter. He began to reach for it, but thought better of it, and closed the cabinet.

Someone knew it was there.

Someone was watching him.

According to the phone caller, it was Meredith.

He was, whether he liked it or not, a part of this game now, and he needed to stay on top of things. He rubbed his hands over his old face, then turned from the cabinet and straightened his tie. Whoever was watching would get suspicious if he got rid of the camera, so it would stay there for now. He exited his office and marched towards the holding cells.

Parker was slumped over, still unconscious and tied to a chair that was bolted and welded to the floor. He was bound with nylon tie-down straps, since that was the strongest thing they could find. Bradley approached and nodded to one of the three officers.

"Okay then, let's wake him up. We don't have time to wait for answers," Bradley said. One of the officers stepped forward with a small vial of smelling salts, and wafted it under Parker's nose. In a few seconds he sat up straight and looked around wildly.

"Welcome back, Agent Parker," Bradley said.

"What did you do? Why am I tied to this chair? Untie me that's an order!" Parker shouted.

"You don't have authority to give me orders, and as I take it, you never did." Bradley pulled up a chair and sat down across from Parker. "These three officers have orders, though, I gave it to them. To shoot you if you should try to escape from that seat. So why don't you and me have a little talk about who you are, and why you're really here."

Parker glared at Bradley at first, but then his face turned into a twisted smile as his lips curled back revealing his perfect white teeth. "Do you think you know what's happening here, old man?" Parker taunted.

"No," Bradley shot back. "I haven't the foggiest clue, which is why you're going to enlighten me."

"Nothing you do will matter, once we locate the General. You heard what that crackpot Vegas quack said about what happened. That's only a taste of his true power. Once we find him you're going to wish you could kill me," Parker hissed.

"Are you sure about that? Because the way I remember it you were pretty terrified in that interrogation room with him. You could hardly hold still."

"I was excited," Parker spat. "I haven't seen the General in years. I thought he was dead. We all did."

"Who's we? You mean you and Ms. Brown?" Bradley asked, raising an eyebrow. Parker looked past Bradley at the other three officers, then up at the light, then back at Bradley.

"Sorry, I can't spoil the surprise. But you will find out. Since you helped us so much so far, I'll leave you alive." Parker's eyes began to darken, and Bradley stood up and moved to a waiting table where another three syringes sat.

"If you're going to go all black-eyed on me, you're going to take another nap," Bradley said, grabbing a syringe. Then he paused and grabbed a second one.

"Uh, Lieutenant, a human dose shouldn't be more than one shot, sir," one of the officers said.

"I'm not entirely sure this *is* a human," Bradley replied, and stuck both needles in Parker's neck. A few moments later his eyes closed and head drooped to one side. "I want two guards on him at all times. No one touches him otherwise." With that, Bradley left the room and pulled out his phone. He dialed briefly and waited for the automated line to answer.

"You've reached Homeland Security…"

Chapter 6
Pit Stop Service

As their truck approached the Arizona, New Mexico border, Donovan could make out multiple cars up ahead on the highway. He squinted his eyes to try and focus, and could see flashing red and blue lights on the vehicles. His heart skipped a beat and he reached over and shook Joe, who had been sleeping since the accident.

"Joe. Joe! Wake up! We've got trouble up ahead," Donovan said, shaking Joe's arm vigorously. Joe reluctantly sat up and pulled his hat off his face, then looked over at Donovan with a sense of agitation.

"I wuh-wuh-was having a good dream," he muttered. "What's the problem?" Joe looked ahead and rubbed his sleep filled eyes, then sat back in his chair. "Uh oh."

"Yeah, uh oh. What are we going to do now?" Donovan asked, looking around the desert but there was no clear path to leave the highway and go around the upcoming roadblock. He slowed the truck as a line had formed ahead of them while police checked vehicles and spoke with drivers and passengers alike.

"What do we do? I can't just, move police cars and throw cops into the air."

"Why not? You did b-back in Las Vegas," Joe shrugged.

"Not this time. Hurry up and tell me, do I have some wonderful hidden convenient power that was my 'specialty' I can use right now? Because if they see us we're done. There's no way my face isn't plastered all over every police broadcast in the country by now."

"Maybe you can burn them?" Joe asked.

"Burn them? I can burn people!?"

"Yeah, it was—"

"Let me guess, my specialty?" Donovan looked at Joe incredulously and Joe smiled innocently back.

"Yes! You're remembering!"

"This isn't helpful, Joe. We need to do something or I have no idea what's going to happen but it won't be good."

The cars moved ahead slowly, and Donovan pulled the truck up a little at a time, until they were third in line for inspection. There was a considerable line of vehicles behind them now, that had built up rather fast. The current car moved forward, and everyone rolled on, making Donovan and Joe next in line to be inspected.

"Anything? Anything at all?" Donovan whispered.

"Why are we whispering now?" Joe whispered back. Donovan rolled his eyes and pulled the truck forward, then rolled down the window as a heavily armed, and heavily armored, officer stepped up to the window.

"What's going on officer? Is everything okay?"

"License and registration please," the officer said.

"Umm, is there some kind of trouble?" Donovan asked.

"Routine check. I need to see your license and registration please," the officer said, holding out his hand. Donovan nodded and reach for his wallet, glancing at Joe when suddenly another officer approached the passenger side and tapped on the window. Donovan hit the button to roll down Joe's window.

"Where are you headed?" She asked Donovan, as Joe leaned back to not block her view.

"Albuquerque," Donovan lied.

"Do you have any identification on you?" The female officer asked, one hand sliding to her sidearm.

"We need to be able to check your I.D. against a wanted fugitive," the first officer said.

"Wanted fugitive?" Donovan could almost feel the beads of sweat rolling down his sideburns.

"I'll be right back," the first officer said, as he took Donovan's license and walked toward one of the cruisers. Donovan slid his foot casually from the brake and hovered over the accelerator. He was prepared to floor it while at least one cop was occupied, and hope that the other didn't have time to draw her gun while they fled.

The female officer watched Donovan like a hawk, her hand resting on her sidearm. It was almost like she didn't even blink.

Look away. Look away. Look away. Donovan repeated over and over in his head. Then the impossible happened. She turned her head to look at her partner as he strode back to the truck, calm and collected.

"All clear, you're free to move on," the officer said as he approached the window and handed Donovan's license back to him. "Thank you for your cooperation, sorry for the delay."

Donovan took the license and nodded, then rolled up both windows as he put the truck in gear. Joe smiled warmly and waved at the female officer as they pulled away slowly, trying not to seem in a big hurry.

Ten minutes passed as they drove in silence before Donovan shook his head and finally spoke. "They didn't check our registration."

"No they didn't," Joe replied.

"I got flagged for sure."

"Yes you d-d-did."

"And now they know exactly where we are, and what road we're taking."

"Buh-but they don't know where we're going," Joe added with a shrug.

"It won't matter. They'll be swooping down on us before we get there. Maybe we need to find a place to lay low. Motel or something and leave in the middle of the night. What do you think?"

Joe looked over at Donovan with a completely shocked look on his face. It took a minute of silence before Donovan looked over for an answer and saw the dumbfounded expression on his partners face.

"What?" Donovan asked.

"You're the General. You have to decide what we do. Not me. I'm just a puh-puh-peon," Joe said. Donovan deflated. He truly had no idea what he was doing, and certainly didn't feel like he had any type of a plan. So, they simply kept driving, Donovan's eyes watching every sign in hopes of finding something that might help them.

Agent Miller checked his phone and nodded, then put it back in his pocket and turned towards Meredith.

"No sightings so far at any of our checkpoints," he screamed over the noise of the helicopter. "Once he crosses the border he's bound to be picked up."

"Are we certain he's heading for New Mexico?" Meredith asked. "There are a lot of places he could hide along the reservations in Arizona."

"No idea. But we did get an ID on the truck he's driving. One witness jotted it down at the accident near Flagstaff. The truck is registered to a body shop in Henderson. *Joe's Bodywerx.*"

"Was it reported stolen?"

"That's just the thing, it wasn't," Miller said. "So either he has some connection to the place, or he's getting help from someone. Either way, we got him."

"If he's still on the 40, we'll catch up with him soon," Meredith said, as she pulled a microphone attached to her headset down to her mouth. "Stay on the current heading," she said into the microphone.

"Yes ma'am," the pilot replied, and Meredith turned back towards Miller. "What's the FBI's plan with this guy?"

"Ascertain his whereabouts, isolate him from the general public if we can, and hit him with enough tranquilizers to bring down an elephant. He's got a lot of questions to answer," Miller shouted. Meredith nodded.

"The Bureau can have what's left when I'm done with him," she said.

"It's not going to work that way. FBI and Homeland get him first, then your super secret group can have him once he's tried, sentenced, and put away," Miller said, leaning closer to Meredith. "If you want to disappear him after he's in a cage, be my guest. But the Justice Department gets him first."

Meredith smiled cordially, then sat back in her seat, her eyes still locked onto Miller. "Of course," she said, with an unnerving smile. Miller sat back and turned to look out the window, unable to bear the creepy feeling he got when he looked into Meredith's eyes.

Only a few minutes had passed but Donovan's uneasiness had gotten the better of him. He continually checked his rearview mirror, paranoid that a police cruiser would be on them any moment and he'd be hauled back to jail. But no lights came in the distance, and no cruiser followed. Still, he thought it best they get off the road for a while.

Up ahead he finally spotted a motel and mechanic shop, so he steered into the parking lot in the back of the building, and the two got out of the truck. Joe stretched while Donovan looked for the motel lobby and desk clerk. Inside was a television in the corner of a rundown, old lobby, whose paint had seen better days. The television was tuned to a sports channel playing a golf tournament, so Donovan surmised he was safe.

He rang the counter bell and waited, then noticed another, smaller television behind the counter on a shelf. The volume was turned down but a news report was playing. Before he could pay closer attention, a scrawny man in jeans and a stained undershirt appeared from a back room.

"Hola. You need room?" The man asked in a thick Hispanic accent.

"Yes, please. One room, two beds if you have it," Donovan forced a smile but his eyes kept checking the television. The man opened up a laptop and whistled while he found a room and completed the check-in procedures. Donovan watched the television as inconspicuously as he could, when suddenly his face showed up on the screen.

The anchor was talking about something he couldn't hear, the volume was much too low, but his face was plastered all over the screen. He glanced up at the clerk, who was too busy on the laptop, but Donovan noticed the room keys hanging on the wall behind the clerk. He would have to turn around to grab them, and when he did...

Donovan raised a shaking left hand to brush his hair back, and as he lowered his hand, he quickly and somewhat awkwardly, swiped his hand from right to left.

The television changed channels.

The clerk saw the hand gesture, and turned to look at the television, which was now playing the golf channel. The clerk smiled and nodded.

"You play?" He asked.

"Not really," Donovan croaked as his dry tongue stuck to the roof of his mouth. "More of a spectator." The clerk grinned and turned to grab a key off the wall, then handed it to Donovan.

"Room 1-0-6. That's seventy-five for the one night, unless you need more," the clerk said.

"One night is fine." Donovan opened his wallet and counted out the bills, then grimaced as he only had fifty dollars in cash on him. The clerk raised an eyebrow.

"We take Visa, Mastercard, AMEX. No Discover."

Donovan nodded and pulled out his credit card and handed it to the clerk. It was a risk, he knew, but he needed rest and this seemed like the only option.

After paying the man and getting the key, Donovan quickly made his way back outside to find Joe standing near the mechanic shop.

"I got us a room. We should get some rest for a few hours and hit the road by nightfall," Donovan said, but Joe wasn't paying attention.

"I ran a sh-sh-shop like this," Joe said. "I really liked it. I liked fixing things. It made me th-think that I could be fixed too, if I found the right mechanic." Joe turned and gave Donovan a small, innocent grin.

"I... I don't know exactly what you think is wrong with you, Joe. But if I can help, once I get my situation squared away..."

"It's ok. You'll remember and you'll help me remember. I know you can," Joe replied solemnly.

"What makes you so sure I can do all these things?"

"Because," Joe patted Donovan on the arm, "you're the General. It's your specialty."

"Maybe I can help you?" A man asked from behind a truck that was up on a lift. He walked around the truck and wiped his hands on a towel.

"No thank you, we're good," Donovan replied.

"Of course you are," the mechanic said. "General," he added. Donovan paused and half turned to face the man.

"I think you have me confused for someone else," Donovan said as he started to walk away.

"I don't think so. I'd recognize you anywhere. Even with that wild haircut you got going on there," the mechanic crossed his arms and spat on the ground. "Thought you were dead."

"Look, we don't want any trouble," Donovan held up his hands and began to back away. The mechanic chuckled.

"Now I *know* that's a lie. The only thing you *ever* wanted was trouble, General."

"He's a bad man," Joe muttered, as he started to slink away from the mechanic shop. "We should go."

"Yeah no kidding," Donovan said to himself. "Just stay back, and leave me alone, okay?"

"No can do. I've been waiting for this for a long time. She told me you'd be around here, but honestly I didn't think I'd find you. Thought you were smarter than to be found," the mechanic said.

"She?"

"You know, I never did get the chance to spar with you. See if you're as good as they say you were. Whaddya think? A few rounds? Best two outta three?"

"Just let us go, and it'll be like we were never here. You can even—ow!" Donovan winced as a wrench flew across the air from the workbench and hit him square on the shoulder.

"Come on, now!" The mechanic yelled. "One round, then. I promise to go easy on you just this once."

Donovan rubbed his shoulder and glared at the mechanic. "Leave us alone. This is your last warning," he said through gritted teeth.

"Now that's more like it," the man cracked his neck from side to side. "You ready?" The mechanic taunted. Donovan looked down at the wrench, then at the mechanic. The wrench suddenly flew through the air towards the mechanic, who lazily dodged it as it clanked against the back wall.

"That it? That's all you got?" The mechanic grinned.

"What's your name?" Donovan asked.

"Pyotr, why?"

"Because I'd feel really bad about kicking your butt when we haven't even been introduced," Donovan said, eyes darting around the mechanic shop behind Pyotr. Donovan winked and a dozen screwdrivers took flight from the toolbox on the workbench and hurled towards Pyotr. With expert timing, he dodged the first few and then tossed his hands in the air, and knocked the rest to the ground.

Donovan winced as that too familiar pain came creeping up the back of his skull.

"Warmups, huh? Okay, I'm game," Pyotr said with a smile and started swinging his arms as though he were throwing objects at Donovan. Lug nuts began flying through the air, somewhat lazily, towards Donovan, and he dodged and ran began a parked car to find cover.

"Oh come on now, General! You need to come out and fight like a man if you want me to fight fair too. Otherwise all bets are off!" Pyotr watched as Donovan slowly stood from his hiding spot, then came back around the car.

"Fine. Fair? How's this for fair?" Donovan held his hands to his sides and focused hard. His head felt like it was splitting open but he kept his eyes on Pyotr and gritted his teeth. Slowly the sand and dirt around him began to rise into the air about halfway up his body.

"Woohoo! Now we're talking! That's some trick!" Pyotr laughed. "Won't do you any good though." Pyotr made a similar motion with his hands, except instead of sand and dirt, oil from several oil pans began to rise like greasy black snakes, and slithered in the air towards Donovan. Donovan thrust his hands forward, causing the thick cloud of sand to shoot towards Pyotr.

"Nice! Very nice!" Pyotr focused his oil snakes to cross in the air, and created a semi shield. The sand and dirt hit the oil and mixed, becoming heavier than Pyotr could manage. The mixture of sludge fell to the ground. Pyotr looked up just as a tire came careening towards him. The surprise shocked him and the tire struck him in the chest, knocking him back and onto the ground.

"I told you, you leave me alone!" Donovan shouted, advancing through the dust in the air.

"Not bad, General!" Pyotr coughed. "Not bad at all. But I'm not beaten yet." Pyotr stood to his feet, staring down Donovan, as a dark curtain seemed to draw over his eyeballs, making them as black as the oil. Suddenly from either side, two cars slid across the gravel towards Donovan.

He held out both hands and caught them, each by their hoods, but they slowly continued to close on him, as though they would pinch him between them both.

"You see, *General*, while you ran like a coward, I continued to train," Pyotr said, his upper lip twitching. "Just… like… you…taught me!"

"I… don't know who…you are…" Donovan groaned, the force driving him to his knees as he focused his mind as much as he could.

"Yes, you do! You turned us into this, and then you just disappeared! And now you're back and what? You think you can just go back to how things were?!"

"You're… insane…" Donovan looked beyond Pyotr, desperately trying to find something to latch onto.

"You know what? Maybe I won't wait for her after all. Maybe I'll just end you myself. You're so weak, we wouldn't want you back anyway!"

"Pyotr…"

"What?!"

"You… talk too much…" The hanging cable from the car lift shot out and wrapped around Pyotr's neck tightly, then yanked him back under the lift itself. The surprise broke his concentration, and the cars stopped their advance, giving

Page 81

Donovan a single moment to act. He reached up with both hands and thrust them downwards, causing the car lift to groan, snap, and the truck overhead to come crashing down.

Right on top of Pyotr.

Donovan fell to his knees, physically and mentally exhausted. He felt like he had just completed a marathon, and lost, while his head was throbbing in pain. He sat back on his heels just so he could keep his body upright, and looked at the destruction all around him.

Multiple people from the motel had come out to see what the noise was, as well as the motel clerk. He heard gasps and murmurs and someone said something about calling 9-1-1, but it was hard for Donovan to make sense of it. A woman noticed him kneeling between the two cars and rushed over.

"Are you okay?" She asked gently, inspecting Donovan as he groggily looked up at her. "Were you in an accident?"

Donovan nodded. "Yes. Something like that," he said slowly. The woman looked to the gathering crowd then back to him.

"I'll be right back, let me see if the hotel has any first aid kits. I'll be right back, don't try to get up," she said. Donovan gave her a weak thumbs up. As she darted off he looked up and saw Joe sit up from the back of the truck that had landed on Pyotr. He looked around and saw Donovan, then smiled and waved innocently. Donovan would have laughed at the situation, but his brain was still disconnected from the rest of him, so doing anything other than not passing out was a chore.

"Did you g-g-get him?" Joe hollered, as he hopped out of the truck bed and slowly sauntered over to where Donovan still sat on the ground. Donovan looked up at Joe and made a face.

Page 82

"There's a truck on top of him. Pretty sure I got him," he said slowly.

"Good," Joe smiled, "then we need to leave. Cops are coming to see wh-what happened. We can't let you get caught." Joe bent over and took Donovan by the armpits and lifted him off the ground like he didn't weight a pound. He pulled Donovan's arm over his shoulder and headed for their truck, which was parked out of view of the gawking crowd. Joe opened the passenger door with a wave of his hand and tossed Donovan onto the bench seat.

"I can drive..." Donovan said, slurring his words.

"You talk worse than me," Joe chuckled, as he hopped behind the wheel. "I drive."

"You don't...have a license..."

"S-s-sure I do. How do you think I puh-puh-picked you up before?" Joe laughed again, put the truck into gear and peeled out of the gravel parking lot.

They headed East, towards their destination, and hadn't been on the road two minutes when they passed two police cars, lights flashing and driving like the devil. Luckily, the cops inside were too busy responding to what witnesses said 'looked like a bomb went off'. Donovan was nearly passed out on the seat, murmuring something as Joe drove on.

Chapter 7
Memories of White Sands

"We're two minutes out, ma'am," the helicopter pilot said over the radio. Meredith didn't bother responding, she already knew too well that they were arriving too late. It had been seventeen minutes since they caught notice of a "bomb" that went off at a local mechanic shop off US-60 in New Mexico. Witnesses described tools flying through the air before a truck fell on the mechanic. Meredith knew exactly what really happened.

She lazily glanced over to Agent Miller, who seemed eager to get on the ground and see what was going on. He wasn't aware that she already had men on the ground all over, and that the first was likely already gone. But there was a lot Agent Miller didn't know, anyway, and Meredith was content to keep it that way. If the FBI started digging in too deep, they would find things they were never supposed to see, and Meredith didn't need any more interference.

She was taking a risk as it was, but so far her plan was working. Except for this one major hiccup that is. She wasn't sure exactly who had engaged with O'Connell, and she was itching to find out who tangled with the General, and lost.

The helicopters touched down on the highway itself, stopping the sparse amount of traffic on US-60, as Meredith, Miller, and a handful of S.W.A.T. disembarked. There were already two police cruisers on the scene, and one of the officers walked up to greet them, curiously.

"I'm Deputy Sheriff Taylor. Who might you be?"

"I'm Meredith Brown, CID, and this is Agent Miller with the FBI," Meredith said, her painted on smile in full effect as the helicopters lifted off behind them.

"FBI? What's this about? We haven't reported anything to the FBI or the... where did you say you're from?" Sheriff Taylor pushed back his cowboy hat and rested his hands on his hips.

"We've been tracking a wanted criminal," Miller began, "and we have reason to believe he has been through here very recently."

"Well you missed the show. I don't know if it's the same person, but somebody made a right mess of the mechanic shop here. Then he jumped in a pickup and took off East. Anything you can tell me about your perp?" Meredith smiled warmly to Sheriff Taylor and handed him a card.

"We're taking over your crime scene, Sheriff. You can call this number if you have any questions. Where was that mechanic shop you mentioned?" Meredith said with a grin. Sheriff Taylor looked at the card, pushed his hat back, and eyed her closely for a minute.

"You don't have any jurisdiction here," he said sternly.

"As a matter of fact," Miller said, stepping between the sheriff and Meredith, "we have jurisdiction everywhere. Why don't you and I come over here and chat while Ms. Brown checks on that shop? Hmm?" Miller put his arm around Sheriff Taylor's shoulder and guided him away. Meredith was pleased.

Good. I've got him around my little finger, she thought.

She walked around the back of the motel where the mechanic shop was, and the moment she cleared the corner of the building she knew exactly what had happened.

Meredith pinched the bridge of her nose and carefully stepped over tools and car parts that were lying everywhere as she made her way to the inside of the shop.

She approached the pickup that had once been raised on the lift, but obviously had fallen. The front tires were at an odd angle, likely from a broken axel, so the truck had probably fallen quickly, and with some assistance.

"So, he's waking up then," she said, stooping down to look at the pool of blood coming from the underside of the truck. She peered at what was left of the man's face, crushed by the weight of the truck, and grunted to herself. "So this is where you were hiding, Pyotr." She clicked her tongue and stood up straight. "Sorry, Pyotr. Once they find you it won't be long before they start asking questions."

Meredith looked around the shop and spotted several oil cartons on a shelf. "That'll do." She held out her hand and, giving a quick look over her shoulder, focused on the oil cartons. Her eyes slowly darkened, red like thick blood, as she stared at the cartons with her hand outstretched.

Suddenly a stream of fire shot out from her palm like a bottle rocket and struck the cartons. Instantly they were ignited, and began to burn hot and bright. She waved another hand and some of the fire seemed to jump from the shelf over to the office, breaking the glass window and igniting a stack of papers and receipts on the desk.

In moments the entire inside of the shop was in flames, and Meredith stood back and admired her handiwork. Her eyes returned to normal as she turned and took in a deep breath.

"Fire! Someone help! The shop is on fire!" She shouted, mimicking panic the best she could. Sheriff Taylor, Agent Miller, and a handful of S.W.A.T. officers all came running around the building to see the mechanic shop now completely engulfed in flames.

"What on Earth?" Sheriff Taylor said, grabbing his radio. "Dispatch, we need the fire department to Red Hill motel right away. Repeat we've got a hot one cookin' here."

"Ms. Brown are you all right?" Miller asked, taking Meredith by the arm. He paused, and looked down, feeling a strong heat coming from her wrist. "Did you get burned?"

"No, no I got too close when it all went up. I think I saw some loose cable sparking right before everything just burst into flames," Meredith said, fanning herself and pulling her arm loose from Miller. "Sheriff is this your idea of a joke? I could have been killed."

"No ma'am, I can assure you we inspected everything in this shop before you arrived," Taylor said.

"Did you now? And what about the body?"

"The body?"

"Yes, the one turning to ash stuck under that pickup truck. You did see and log the body, didn't you?" Meredith squinted her eyes as she felt their color changing.

Miller looked from Taylor to Meredith and for a moment swore he could see the fire dancing in her eyes.

"Where was the body, Ms. Brown?" Miller asked.

"See the lift? Right under there. I noticed the blood and I got closer to peek in. Sure enough, a man dead under there." She turned to face Sheriff Taylor, "Sheriff I want a full report of everything you found here. As far as I'm concerned, this is the work of an arsonist."

"An arsonist? Are you sure?" Miller raised an eyebrow looking at Meredith.

"I firmly believe someone was trying to cover up a murder," Meredith said, then walked away back towards the
Page 88

front. Miller followed quickly to catch up and tried to talk to her out of earshot of everyone else.

"Ma'am, do you think O'Connell had anything to do with this?" He asked.

"Agent Miller," Meredith began without stopping, "that man under the truck was my deep cover agent. I'm positive O'Connell came through here. And I have no doubt he tired to burn this place to the ground to cover the evidence."

"*Your* deep cover agent? Why didn't you say anything?" Miller stopped and grabbed Meredith by the shoulder, turning her to face him. She looked at his hand, then at him menacingly.

"What do you think 'deep cover' means, exactly?"
*** Miller grimaced as she pulled her shoulder away from his hand and walked back towards where the helicopters had landed away from the highway.

"We're not getting any closer by waiting around here, Agent Miller!" Meredith shouted over her shoulder at him. He scoffed and pulled out his phone, typed a quick message and hit send before he marched after Meredith.

White Sands, New Mexico was as close to a desert wasteland as Donovan had ever seen. As far as he could tell there was nothing but small rolling hills of very blindingly white sand, articulated by a mountain range in the distance. He held a hand to his face and squinted his eyes so much he hardly could see anything at all. It made him wish he had grabbed a pair of sunglasses.

He and Joe had abandoned the truck two miles ago off the side of the road, and made their way on foot until they reached an old, long since abandoned rest stop near a closed

Page 89

hiking trail. The structure was not more than a pair of concrete "T"s, connected in the middle to create shade, and two crude bathrooms within, separated by an interior concrete wall. The two men huddled in the shade as they planned their next move.

"Joe," Donovan said as patiently as he could muster, "this is a national park. There's no way some secret government plot was carried out in a national park." He waved one arm out. "There are hiking trails. That means there are people."

"Not that way," Joe pointed north with a smile.

"That way? Joe, that's a missile testing range. And that's like, eight miles away."

"Nine p-p-point six eight miles," he replied. Donovan stared blankly at him.

"We can't walk nine miles in the blazing hot sun, over White Sands. We'll cook to death before we find anything!" Donovan sighed as exasperatedly as he could and crumpled to the ground, his back against the concrete. "This is hopeless."

"Y-you can do it though," Joe smiled down. "I know you can."

"What? Walk nine miles in one hundred degree heat? Thank you for the vote of confidence but I doubt that very much."

"It was—"

"Don't," Donovan interrupted. "Don't you dare say walking nine miles was my specialty." Joe, grinned, his body began to convulse, then he exploded with roaring laughter, doubling over.

"Specialty!? Walking?! General you're f-fun-funny!" Donovan wasn't amused, but he couldn't help but crack a smile as his traveling companion continued to roar, perhaps a little too loud though.

"Ok, ok. Quiet down, someone will hear you," he said as he got back to his feet with some effort. "Seriously, we need to have at least some idea of where we're go—"

Joe stopped laughing in an instant and grabbed Donovan by the lapels of his shirt, then thrust his back against the concrete structure so hard he nearly knocked the wind out of him.

"Where?!" Joe demanded. "Where are we going?" He pulled Donovan away from the wall and slammed him back against it a second time.

"Agh! Joe! What the hell?! What are you doing?" Donovan tried to break the larger man's grip on him, but he got thrust against the wall again for his efforts.

"Where, General?! W-wha-where?! What's our h-heading?" Donovan stared Joe in the face, shocked, and more than a little scared. Then he saw it, just the same as the mechanic back at the hotel and shop. Joe's eyes darkened, like ink had filled them from the inside. They went completely black, shiny, but dark as night.

"Joe… you need to let go of me, right… now," Donovan demanded, but Joe wasn't listening.

"What are your orders, G-G-General?" Joe swiftly moved his hands from the lapels of Donovan's shirt, and placed them under his armpits. He lifted Donovan off the ground so effortlessly Donovan might as well have been a small child.

"Joe!" Donovan shouted, but he was helpless. He lifted Donovan up and right into the path of the blazing sun, that blinded him. He raised a hand to block the light, then everything went white, like the sands themselves bounced the light

Page 91

of the sun directly into his eyes. Amid the blinding brightness stood a rounded concrete dome, not much bigger than the restroom structure. There was the door and the strange logo he had seen before. But then off in the distance, he heard a strange whistle, followed by a massive explosion that was somehow brighter than the white light all around. He felt the heat and a rush of hot wind and sand gust into his face. He tried to close his eyes, but he couldn't.

The light enveloped the dome, and the door, and Donovan, and his feet struck onto the hard concrete ground. He blinked and there before him stood Joe, a strange grin on his meaty face, his eyes back to normal.

"I see. So we d-d-do have to go north then. Better get a drink first," Joe sauntered over to an old water fountain that looked like it hadn't worked in a decade. He pressed the silver button and a small but sure stream of water came out of the old fountain.

"What… what did you just do to me?" Donovan asked, his legs trembling beneath him as he fought to keep balance. His head began to hurt, but not as bad as before. Enough that he squinted his eyes from the pain, but he didn't feel like collapsing. At least not yet.

"Hmm? Oh, I helped jog your m-memory," Joe answered as though he had just walked his dog rather than reach into Donovan's skull.

"My memory? You jogged my memory? You can do that?" Donovan stumbled over to the fountain and nearly fell but Joe caught him and set him straight on his feet again.

"Not like you… it was…"

"My specialty. Well why can't you make me remember what happened at the casino? Or to my wife? Or why I was in the military?!"

Joe shrugged.

"You didn't ask me to," he said.

Donovan's jaw dropped. He tried to form a sentence but all that came out was a strained grunt, like his vocal chords had stopped working. He stared at his companion and finally looked away and shook his head. He felt a heavy hand land on his shoulder, and looked back at Joe, who smiled.

"Once we g-get there, you will remember everything. Then you can fix everything," he said calmly. Donovan sighed hard and long, then nodded and slowly pushed Joe's big hand off his shoulder.

"Right, let's get on with it then," he muttered, and started towards the blazing hot sand.

Chapter 8
Blindsight

Phones were ringing nonstop in the LVPD bullpen, as everyone from Henderson to Summerlin and everywhere in between was calling with new information about Donovan, in hopes of snatching up the cash reward for his capture. Of course it was all nonsense, and Lieutenant Bradley knew that. Nevertheless it was good to keep the man's face plastered on every screen in the Southwest as the manhunt continued, and especially since Bradley didn't know who he could trust anymore.

He sat at his desk poring over new notes and sighing with each page turned, when his cell phone vibrated on his desk.

"What now?" He muttered to himself as he turned the phone over to look at the screen. His eyebrow raised when he saw the message was from Special Agent Miller. "What have you got for me, Miller?" He muttered to himself, as he opened it to read the message. But before his eyes focused on the words, another officer knocked on the door.

"What is it?" Bradley growled.

"Sir, there's a survivor from the casino attack that just woke up. You should head down there sir," the officer said in a hurry.

"Why is that?" Bradley asked as he twisted left and right to crack his back.

"She claims to be the wife of Donovan O'Connell."

Bradley squinted at the officer. "Can we confirm that intel? Or is this another loon trying to cash in on the reward?"

"I thought that too, until her attending doctor sent me a photo, and it's a near perfect match with the footage from the casino. The woman seen with Donovan before the attack." The Officer came closer and produced his phone and handed it to Bradley to inspect. He put his reading glasses on and peered at the screen, then picked up a printed paper with both Donovan and the woman with him.

"Hmmm," he growled. "You're driving."

"Where is she?" Bradley asked the nurse with about the same amount of tact as a bulldog going after a bone.

"Uh, let me look," the nurse said, obviously stalling.

"We called ahead, the patient claiming to be Mrs O'-Connell," Bradley said, very matter of factly.

"Oh right, that patient. Room thirty six zero two," the nurse smiled and turned to walk away.

"Did you post a guard?" The officer asked as he and Bradley marched down the hallway.

"The moment I got word. If she is who she says she is, I want answers and I don't want anyone from any other department talking to her before we do," Bradley said. "And that goes for the press, too," he grunted. "What's your name, son?"

"Wilco, sir."

"Well, Wilco, you let me do the talking in there, just keep an eye out, got it?" Officer Wilco nodded his agreement as the two of them turned a corner and stopped cold. There before them was a dozen reporters gathered outside one of the hospital rooms.

"Let me guess," Wilco began, "that's room thirty six oh two?"

"Dammit," Bradley moaned. They marched ahead and before they came within fifty feet the press noticed and turned their attention towards the pair.

"Lieutenant! Is it true? Is this Donovan O'Connell's wife?!"

"Any chance of catching O'Connell this week?"

"Does she have information about the attack?"

"Is she an accomplice or…"

"Let us through!" Bradley bellowed, his voice echoed in the hallway. "You can ask our media relations department, now get out of my way or I'll have you charged with obstruction!" He knew the threat was bogus, but it had the desired effect of clearing a path to the room. Once they had reached the door, two officers that had been stationed at the entrance stood aside and let the men slip in.

Laying in bed was Kathy, a bandage around her head that covered her right eye. She had bruises on her right cheek and her left arm was in a sling. Officer Wilco paused before continuing but Bradley marched to the bed, albeit a little more relaxed.

"Ma'am," he started and she turned her head to look at them both with her one uncovered eye.

"Yes," Kathy said weakly, "before you ask, yes, Donovan is my husband." Bradley nodded and pulled up a chair, while Officer Wilco turned an uneasy eye towards the door.

"Mrs. O'Connell, we need to talk to you about your husband," Bradley said softly. "Is there anything you can tell us that might help us locate him?"

"Locate him?" Kathy furrowed her eyebrow. "You mean you don't have him in custody?" Both men looked at each other.

"Ma'am, your husband escaped custody a few days ago. He's been on the run," Bradley said.

Kathy sighed. "Do you have any idea where he is?"

"Any help you might give us would greatly improve our chances of locating and subduing your husband," Officer Wilco interjected. Bradley shot him a look.

"The sooner we find your husband, the better it will be for everyone," Bradley continued as he tried his best to smile at Kathy.

"Honestly, I have no idea where he could be," Kathy said as she looked away. "I assume you tried our house?"

"He's… currently not in the State, ma'am," Bradley said quietly, with the full knowledge that the reporters outside had gone very quiet, and were likely trying to eavesdrop.

"I don't understand," Kathy looked at the men confused. "Surely he couldn't have gotten that far."

"He had help. But we don't know from whom," Bradley held up his phone with a surveillance camera shot of the old pickup truck. "We haven't identified him, yet. Someone was driving an old pickup truck when your husband escaped the precinct."

Kathy swallowed hard and reached a shaking hand for her cup of water nearby. After taking a sip and clearing her throat, she continued.

"Do you at least know *where* he's headed?" She asked hoarsely.

"He was last seen in Arizona, near Flagstaff, headed East. We don't know where he going," Bradley said.

"Near Flagstaff," Kathy repeated as she took a deep breath and closed her one eye. "He's…" her eyelid fluttered, her hands clenched into fists, and then she gasped. "He's in New Mexico."

"Message from Bradley" Miller shouted over the noise of the helicopter at Meredith. "Says he has a source claiming O'Connell is in New Mexico." She nodded as she looked at something on her tablet, but held it and just the right angle to avoid letting Miller see what it was.

"That's a lot of ground. Did he say where?" she shouted back.

"That's all I've got. Any ideas?"

"There are a few places he might run to. There's a…" she trailed off and looked at Miller in the corner of her eye before adjusting her microphone. "Turn us towards White Sands!" She shouted into the microphone at the pilot.

"White Sands? Are you sure? It's over two hundred square miles," Miller gave Meredith a look.

"Two hundred square miles of bright white dirt, Agent Miller. He'll stick out like a sore thumb, and we'll grab him." Meredith shoved her tablet back into her bag with a smirk on her face. The look was not lost on Miller.

"Tell me what you're thinking," he said.

"I just did. You do your job and I'll do mine," Meredith shot back.

"You know, this would go a lot smoother if you'd share vital information. The FBI would look on your cooperation very highly."

"Would they now?" Meredith smirked again. Her eyes quickly blazed, as though on fire. Miller squinted to look but the effect had gone.

"Whoever you're really working for, I'm sure they could use some credit with us," Miller threw down his trump card, hoping Meredith would take the bait. She merely raised an eyebrow.

"You really don't know a damn thing, do you Miller?" She smiled. "Shame. I was starting to like you." As she looked out the helicopter window, Miller thumbed the holster release on his sidearm. He could read between the lines, and figured if one of them was going for a dive out of the helicopter, it wouldn't be him.

"You know I've been thinking," he started as he shifted in his seat to hide his hand on his pistol. "We might cover more ground if we split up once we get there."

"You read my mind, Miller," Meredith said, still looking the other direction. "Are you sure you're not psychic as well?"

Miller slowly pulled his sidearm from the holster, but he was too slow. Meredith turned, her eyes ablaze, her hand, previously hidden from Miller's sight, was on fire. He hesitated when he saw it, and cursed himself for it, because she thrust her hand against his chest and the next thing he knew his jacket, tie and shirt were on fire.

"Agh!" His shout was lost among the noise of the helicopter. He drew his weapon and fired randomly, puncturing holes in the cabin but missing Meredith by a mile. He grabbed at the door behind him and slid it open, which Meredith took advantage of and kicked him hard in his burning chest, sending him reeling out of the helicopter.

"Let me know what you find, Miller!" Meredith shouted out of the helicopter door before swinging it shut. "Head to the bunker," she said to the pilot. "If he's headed to White Sands, that's exactly where he'll go."

"What exactly would he be looking for in New Mexico?" Bradley leaned forward and steepled his fingers. "Anything you can tell us will be a huge help."

"You don't understand," she said with a quiver in her voice. "You don't *need* to understand. You just have to stop him. Who else knows about all this?"

"It's been out in the open for a few days, the media is all over it. I have an FBI Taskforce looking into it, as well as the local LVPD. There's also a woman claiming to be from the CID on the ground in the area," Miller said as he scrolled through his phone and found a picture. "She says her name is Meredith Brown," he held up the phone for Kathy, and she gasped.

"Oh God," she said. "Oh God oh God," Kathy grimaced. "Her name isn't Meredith Brown, and she's not with anyone you've ever heard of," she swallowed hard.

"Then would you care to enlighten me?" Bradley growled. Kathy took a deep breath, held it a moment too long, then exhaled slowly.

"Donovan is… not my husband. Well he is but… it's complicated," she said quietly.

"I'm going to need you to make it uncomplicated real fast for me, ma'am," Bradley whispered, his upper lip twitched as he tried to contain his frustration.

"Do you… have a coin?" Kathy asked.

"I do!" Officer Wilco piped up, and quickly produced a quarter. He handed it to Kathy who held it up and stared at the coin for a long moment.

"Back in the early 1950s, and late 60s, well I'm sure you've heard of MK Ultra?" Kathy looked at Bradley while she twirled the quarter on the top of her fingers.

"The CIA's attempt at making psychic soldiers. I've heard of it. Who hasn't?" Bradley grunted.

"They didn't attempt it. It worked. But they got caught and Congress stepped in. So, it was decided that the work should go to… the private sector. Away from government oversight. Keep the government blind to what was really happening." Kathy rested the coin in her palm. "Blindsight was born."

The quarter slowly levitated a few inches above Kathy's open palm. It then spun and twirled in mid air as she gently moved her fingers. Officer Wilco stared in disbelief, while Bradley, having had already seen such feats first hand, crossed his arms over his chest.

"So, you're one of them?" He said with a grunt.

"Barely. I can't do what the General can. Not even close. But still…" she flicked her fingers and the quarter flew across the room and stuck hard into the wall. "I can do enough."

"You were telling me about this government group, and how it was connected to O'Connell," Bradley continued. Kathy cleared her throat and nodded.

"Blindsight picked up where the CIA left off, except they had much, much better results. For decades they trained soldiers for black ops in psychic warfare and espionage. Some recruits rose through the ranks. Donovan entered the program as a government liaison, and he showed incredible progress in multiple types of psychic abilities. He's literally one of the rarest the program ever saw. I was his assistant, and eventually his handler.

"But there were others whose specialties were far stronger than Donovan's. Some in pyrotechnics, some in remote viewing, others in manipulating matter."

"Manipulating matter? You're gonna have to dumb that down for me. I'm just a poor dumb cop you know," Bradley raised an annoyed eyebrow at Kathy.

"You'd call it telekinesis. Like what I just did with the quarter, only a thousand times stronger." Kathy pointed to Bradley's phone, and he scrolled to the shot of Meredith again. "Siobhan Donaldson was an expert pyro-kinetic. Pyotr Baranov was one of the best tele-kinetics I ever saw. He could do things with his mind that scared most of us. Except the General. Somehow the General kept a pretty good handle on things."

"What happened to the project?" Officer Wilco blurted out. Kathy took a sip of her water as her eyes fell.

"Jonah. Jonah happened."

"There's got to be hundreds of square miles here," Donovan complained. "How are we going to find one little bunker?"

"We'll f-f-ind it," Joe stammered. "When we do, you can f-f-fix me."

Donovan shrugged and trudged along onto the seemingly endless white plain of sand, with Joe watching him carefully from a few steps behind.

Chapter 9
Here There Be Monsters

"Miller! You've got to keep an eye out for someone else working with O'Connell. Goes by the name Jonah," Bradley shouted into his phone. "Catch them both if you can. Call me!" Bradley ended the call and stormed back into the hospital room. He had ordered the reporters to vacate the hall, and threatened one of the doctors to help him do it, so it was easier to step outside and call Agent Miller.

"Run this by me again," Bradley said as he plopped into the chair by Kathy's hospital bed. "Why call him the "General"?"

"Because he is one," Kathy sat up in her bed as best as she could manage. "Marine Corp General. The CIA insisted some of their own be integrated into Blindsight. So, half was theirs, the other half was ours. The program was privately ran, with minimum interference. The General reported to his people what was happening, what we discovered, new technologies, etcetera."

"Why'd it go belly up?" Bradley asked. "Something to do with this Jonah character?"

"Like I said," Kathy opened her hand and her cup of water gingerly slid across her side table into her waiting palm. "Jonah happened." She took a sip and swallowed with some effort, then continued. "He was put in charge of Blindsight by someone with much higher authority, we assume the CIA but honestly I don't know. He was," Kathy cleared her throat, "ruthless, in his pursuit of perfection."

"Perfection? Of what?" Wilco blurt out. Bradley had given up trying to muzzle the man, so he just let the question linger.

"Making the perfect psychic soldier. And Donovan was as close as they'd come, but there were complications. Donovan, he… he wanted out. After I was assigned to be the General's handler, he and I came up with a plan. Part of that was just to get married to avoid much suspicion. IDs were faked, his connection to the CIA took care of that. All that remained was to, well, wipe his memory of it all."

"Wipe his memory? O'Connell can do that?"

"That and more. He was one of the most talented in the program. And there was absolutely no way Jonah was going to let him leave." Kathy trailed off.

Bradley sat back in his chair, crossed his arms over his chest, and rested his chin in one hand. It was a lot to process, and if he hadn't witnessed some of it all first hand, he wouldn't believe a word of what was being said.

"What became of Jonah?" Bradley asked.

"I thought he died, but honestly I don't know." Kathy said with a twinge of trembling to her voice. "Donovan *did* wipe his own memory, but not everything went to plan. There was… an incident."

"You want to tell me about that?" Bradley leaned forward and raised an eyebrow.

"We're wasting time. You should be out there trying to find him, not listening to all the mistakes that were made," Kathy set her cup down and looked out the window.

"I've got the FBI in my hair, someone claiming to be from Homeland that obviously isn't, and this Siobhan woman all looking for your husband." Bradley shook his head. "I haven't seen one CIA agent though. Gotta admit, I'm a little surprised."

Kathy shook her head. "You won't see them. First of all I doubt they're in play, they'd just disavow everything. Cut their losses and walk away. Secondly, if there is someone from the agency involved, you'll never see them anyway."

"There's another thing that's bothering me," Bradley leaned forward again. "*You* survived the attack at the casino. Want to clue me in how that happened at least?"

"I barely survived," Kathy said, as she looked back at Bradley. "When the General went haywire, I shielded myself from flying debris. Obviously not well enough." She pointed around at her hospital room. "You showed me a picture of Siobhan. Claiming to be who, from where?"

"Meredith Brown, from some department of the Marines. That's obviously a lie, according to you."

"I'll say," Kathy snorted.

"Can you tell me more about her, or is that above my pay grade, too?"

"After the incident, I thought Siobhan was dead, too. She should be."

"One of yours then?"

"Sadly, yes. Like I told you, she can create, control, and manipulate fire."

"You can't be serious," Bradley said, incredulously.

"I am. It was her specialty. The General could do it too, but not like her. Real bad temper. I'm kind of surprised she didn't cook you alive, Lieutenant."

"Thanks," Bradley scoffed.

"Look," Kathy began as she sat up with a groan, "you have got to find him. What happened at the casino is small beans compared to what could be unleashed."

"What are we looking at here? I mean if all goes to hell," Bradley leaned forward even more, and stared Kathy in her one good eye.

"There were a few within Blindsight that wanted to use these, abilities… to cause chaos."

"Why?"

"Because we can. That's why." Kathy leaned back against her pillow again.

"So O'Connell was in charge on one side, this Jonah character in charge of the other, and Meredith who is really Siobhan is looking for O'Connell, while Jonah might be dead, " Bradley shook his head. "Do I have that right?"

"No, Donovan was just the CIA liaison." Kathy took a labored breath and swallowed some water. "Jonah ran every-thing. I never actually met him, only ever heard his voice a few times when I listened in on a phone call. The way he spoke he barely sounded human. All business, no empathy," she said in almost a whisper. She grew silent and after a full minute Bradley stood up.

"If you'll excuse me, Mrs. O'Connell, I have a few phone calls to make." Kathy nodded again and closed her eye as Bradley tapped Officer Wilco on the shoulder, and left the hospital room.

Once out in the hall he breathed a heavy sigh, and turned to Officer Wilco.

"What's the play, Lieutenant?" He asked Bradley.

"Call the station, have them wake up Parker but keep him contained. He and I are going to have a chat."

Donovan blinked and scratched his head as he stared at a small, domed concrete structure with a plain, metal door.

Page 108

Aside from the door, there weren't any other defining features, just a lot of sand and the feeling that whatever this was, it hadn't been visited or used in a very, very long time. He looked to Joe who was almost trembling with either excitement or fear, Donovan couldn't tell which.

"You're sure this is what we're looking for?" He asked Joe, who slowly turned to face him.

"You d-ddon't remember?"

"Not a thing, Joe. That's what I've been telling you for days now. Are you sure, I mean *sure* that this is the place we need to find? It looks like a storage bunker, but certainly not some secret lab." Donovan walked around the dome twice, examined it, and rested his hands on his hips.

"This is it. I k-k-know it is. We just have to get in," Joe said, his voice stuttering a little more than usual. Donovan sighed and grabbed the handle of the rusted door. He tugged on it and tried to open it, but the door refused to budge. He looked over his shoulder at Joe.

"You want to give me a hand here?"

Joe nodded and held out a hand. The door didn't budge. Joe held out both hands, and the door creaked and groaned like it wanted to move, but it still didn't budge. Donovan raised an eyebrow.

"Come one, push a little harder. I've been doing all the work lately." He grinned.

"You try, General," Joe grunted in frustration. Sweat beads were forming on his brow, but he kept straining against the door. Donovan shrugged and held his hands out in the same fashion. He felt the door. The metal, the hinges, the latch, the rust. He could feel the contours of the door frame, the simple lock, and something else.

A weld.

A long, single bead of weld running the entire length of the door, top to bottom. But not from the outside. The door was welded shut from the *inside*.

Donovan relaxed and looked at Joe, then shook his head.

"Hate to break it to you, but we're not getting in here. This door is welded shut."

"We have to," Joe said, still straining.

"But we can't," Donovan insisted.

"We *have* to!" Joe shouted, his stutter gone, his voice somehow different. The door groaned anew, but it still didn't budge. Donovan stepped back and nodded.

"Okay, okay, let me think. So there's this secret door in the middle of nowhere. It has to lead somewhere, right? Probably, underground? I mean, that makes about as much sense as anything else."

"Elevator," Joe said, his voice back to normal.

"Sure, I could see that. But we still can't open the door to get to it if there is one."

"M-m-maybe you could melt it," Joe suggested.

"Melt a metal door?" Donovan nearly laughed.

"You can control fire, it was—"

"My specialty, right. Of course it was." Donovan lolled his head back and sighed out loud. "You realize the melting point of steel is something like… three thousand degrees?"

"You don't need to m-melt the whole door," Joe said with a smile. "Just the hinges." Donovan lowered his head and looked at his simple companion.

"Holy shit, you're right." He said as he approached the door. "The hinges might not be steel. Even if they are we only have to break them loose from the door." He ran his hands along the opposite side of the door from the handle.

"I can't feel any welds. They only welded one side!" Donovan turned to see Joe smiling back, his creepy, slightly disturbing smile.

"Do it! Melt it, G-g-general!" He said excitedly.

"I... how exactly do I do that?" Joe grabbed Donovan's wrist and planted his palm against the edge of the door.

"Think, *fire!*" Joe shouted, demandingly. Donovan, a little shocked, nodded and turned his eyes back to the door.

"Right. Fire. Fire." He muttered to himself. "Fire..." As he stared intently at his hand, he felt a tickle on the back of his neck. A small bead of sweat had formed near his hairline, and was slowly traveling down his neck and under his collar.

"Fire..." he chanted softly, as the sweat began to bead on his brow. "Fire," he grunted a little louder. He could feel heat begin to build on his palm, but he wasn't sure if it was his doing, or just the metal door in the blazing sun.

"Come on... fire... come on," he groaned.

Then his head grew light.

There was ringing in his ears.

The too familiar pain at the base of his skull began to rise anew, like a choir raising their voices to match his own.

"*Fire! Fire!*" He shouted, as Joe began chanting alongside him.

"Fire! F-f-fire!"

The door began to change colors, from rusted red to a bright orange around his hand. Then it was his hand that had turned red too. And the concrete surrounding the doorframe. His whole world was turning rust red. His hand was hot, hotter than he had felt before. He lifted it away from the door but the heat didn't stop. It wasn't coming from the door, it was coming from *him.*

"Fire," he said again, but it came out as more of a growl than before. "*Fire…*"

Then his hand burst into flames. It shocked him at first, scared him. He shook his hand violently trying to put the fire out, but it wouldn't subside. He turned to look at Joe who was smiling a wicked, devilish grin. Everything was red.

Donovan turned back to the door and pressed his flaming palm against the metal. He grunted and growled and felt something softening under his touch. The heat was intense, and he was amazed his flesh wasn't boiling from it. It hurt, more than his aching, splitting head. More than he had felt pain before. Of *course* it hurt! He was literally burning!

Just then something popped from inside the door. He quickly repositioned his hand to the upper part and focused harder. The sweat was pouring down his face.His head was aching so bad he felt like collapsing. He wiped his forehead with his free hand and kept at it. Another loud banging noise.

"That's… two. I think I can't… do much more…" Donovan groaned.

Suddenly he was flung backwards through the air. He tumbled head over heels a few times in the dirt until he came to a stop laying on his back and coughing, having the wind knocked out of him. Superheated air within the dome had found a small pore and blew out with tremendous force, knocking Donovan back and onto the sand. He stared up at the sky, which slowly melted from red to blue again, dotted with small white clouds. His head ached and his ears rang. He raised a trembling hand to see that the fire was out, but his hand looked red as though it had been touching hot iron.

"Let's go, G-general," he heard a distant voice say. His body raised up from the sand and in a moment he found himself slung over Joe's big shoulder. He heard creaking and whining of metal being twisted. Then his world went dark.

———————

Miller opened his eyes and groaned in pain. His back hurt. His hips hurt. His head hurt. But he was alive, at least as far as he could tell. He suddenly remembered being on fire, and sat up quickly, too quickly for the pain in his head, and patted his chest. What was left of his shirt and jacket were scorched, but the Kevlar vest he wore under it all was little worse for wear. He slowly removed his jacket and tore off the remains of his shirt, then carefully felt over his ribs and legs to check for any broken bones.

Whether by luck or divine intervention, nothing seemed to be broken. He stood with some effort and pulled his phone from his pocket. The screen was cracked in two corners, but the lower portions were responsive. He saw a missed call and voicemail from Bradley. He'd have to check it in a few minutes. First he needed to figure out where the hell he was, and try to get a response team headed his way. Someone from the FBI preferably, that he knew and could trust.

As he began to dial, his phone rang. Without hesitation he answered the call. "This is Miller."

"There's an FBI safe house one and a half kilometers from your location. Get there," a man's voice said.

"Excuse me, who is this? How did you get this number?"

"North, Northwest as the crow flies."

"I said who is this? Tell me how you got a federal agent's number!"

"You're wasting time, Agent Miller. If you want to catch up with Ms. Brown you're going to need to get to that safe house. You'll understand when you get there." The call ended just as abruptly as it came through. Miller quickly tried to call back but the number was blocked.

"Damnit," he cursed to himself. He cracked his sore neck and checked the map on his phone, quickly looking for anything that was roughly a kilometer and a half northwest of where he was. The map only showed a gas station, so Miller set the directions on his phone, and headed that way.

Chapter 10
In the Dark

Donovan opened his groggy eyes, instantly regretting it as the bright light of a desk lamp stabbed his retinas with searing pain. Everything hurt. His head was throbbing, his hand felt like it had been scorched, and his back was aching, probably from landing on rocks after being flung back like a rag doll. He held up his other hand against the light and groaned.

"Oh good, you're a w-w-ake," Joe muttered. He lumbered over to Donovan and forcibly opened one eye at a time with his stubby fingers, checking to see if Donovan was conscious.

"Ow! Yes, I'm awake! Turn that damn light off will you!" Donovan whined.

"Can't. Not much else light in here. Everything t-t-turned off," Joe shrugged and left Donovan's side. He sat up with a labored moan and looked around at his surroundings. Sure enough there was hardly much light in the place, wherever they were. Donovan rolled off the table he had been on and groaned when his feet his the concrete floor beneath him.

"Where are we?"

"Lab. Underground. Far, far underground," Joe said. He was making noise in the dark, forcing open filing cabinets and tearing through the contents.

"I gathered that. I meant *where* are we? What is this place?"

Joe turned and looked frustratedly at Donovan. "Lab. Far, far underground," he repeated.

"Got it, thanks," Donovan rolled his eyes and began slowly exploring the place himself. "Why is there no light? Is this place from the 1900s or something?" He didn't expect, or receive a reply from Joe. Assuming his questions were't going to be answered by his simple companion, Donovan continued poking around in the near darkness of the strange facility.

Joe had taken them to some large room, that for some reason made Donovan think of a prison cafeteria. There was a second and third floor with railings but no stairs or elevator that he could see. From what he could tell this was some kind of inescapable pit. But it was clean, with a few desks over-turned and paper scattered all over the floor.

Then something else caught his eye. A file on the floor that had its edges singed. Then another loose paper. And an-other file. He followed the path in the ever dimming light until he hit a wall, quite literally, and backed up. His eyes went wide. There was a scorched outline of a person on the wall. As though something very bright, or very hot, had hit both the wall and the person at the same time.

He looked down at his own hand, it was still a little red from holding fire and burning the hinges of the metal door off. The pain was gone, but the memory was fresh. If he could cre-ate the kind of heat that would melt metal, what else could he do?

"Not you," Joe said, startling Donovan.

"Huh?"

"Not you," he pointed to the wall. "Someone else. Bad lady."

"What bad lady?"

"Bad lady. Come on. We need p-p-power. You can do it." Joe patted Donovan heavily on the shoulder and smiled. Donovan turned to follow.

"I can do what!?"

_____

"Did you wake him up?" Bradley growled as he approached the Interrogation room where Parker was being held.

"Yes but, he's not happy. Are you sure you want to go in there?" An officer asked.

"No, I'm not. But I have to. Unless you want to do the questioning?" The officer shook his head vigorously. "That's what I thought." Bradley scoffed and opened the door.

"You're pretty stupid if you think I'm going to talk," Parker said as Bradley entered and took a seat. Bradley sighed and folded his arms over his chest as nonchalantly as he could manage, given that his heart was racing. He wasn't afraid of anyone at his age, but there was something about these people that made him nervous.

"Oh you don't have to say a word," Bradley smiled.

"Good! Because I'm not...wait, why?" Parker asked, his demeanor slightly changed.

"We've got one of your people... your people? Does that sound wrong? Your people. One of you. Mind reader. We've got a mind reader on the way."

"Like hell you do. You wouldn't know the first thing about people like us."

"You're damn right about that. Fact is you scare me, Parker. It's a good thing I don't have to deal with you," Bradley smiled again, hoping Parker would take the bait.

He did.

"Who said there are people who can read minds?"

"The General did," Parker's eyes flash with a hint of fear.

Gotcha.

Page 117

"He's a fugitive. He's not going to help you even if you did find him."

"We didn't find him. He came back to us. Wants to roll on everything and everyone from Blindsight in exchange for immunity." Parker's face turned five shades of pale. It was all Bradley could do to keep from laughing. He made a thoughtful face and bit down hard on his inner cheek to keep his face from contorting into a smile.

"That… you're lying. He wouldn't do that," Parker swallowed hard, his words barely above a whisper.

"Of course he would!" Bradley couldn't contain the laughter anymore. "He was CIA, or didn't you know that? The whole casino thing was an accident. Gonna be overlooked if he cooperates. He's giving us everything right now. You, Siobhan, everyone."

"*Siobhan*?! Who… who's that?" Parker's eyes turned black again, and he pulled against his restraints. The nylon cord groaned and whined but didn't give.

"Yeah yeah we know it all, now. Ms. Brown had even me fooled for a bit, but not anymore," Bradley picked at his teeth like he was bored.

"You're lying," Parker spat.

"So what is it you do? Are you like the Hulk or something?" Bradley asked, ignoring the accusation. "You get angry and get strong, is that it?"

Parker continued to pull against the restraints but to no avail. Finally he relaxed and heaved a few angry breaths before looking at Bradley again, his eyes having returned to normal.

"So, the great General made a deal huh? Tell you what, Lieutenant, how about you and I made one?" Parker's voice had softened, almost desperate as he clung for control.

"'Bout time you start making sense. But what in the world could you offer that O'Connell can't?"

"I know names. Names the General never knew about. Black sites he never inspected. We hid a lot from him and his government handlers," Parker leaned forward. "Things only his pretend wife knew."

"Kathy is alive. I just finished talking to her myself. Oh she had a lot to say," Bradley teased. "I'll bet my pension you don't got anything she doesn't know."

"I doubt that," Parker smirked. "You give me the same deal the General got, and I'll give you everything."

"How do I know you have anything I want, Parker?"

"Because I know the one black site only two people alive know about. And it's right under this precinct."

Bradley's heart skipped a beat. He knew there was a bead of sweat on the back of his neck and he was willing it not to fall. He raised an eyebrow and swallowed hard.

"Yeah? You and who else knows this?"

Parker grinned his wicked smile. "Just me and Jonah."

Joe held up a small cigarette lighter, the tiny flame flickering in the dark as he felt along the walls. Donovan kept his eyes on the big man, watching intently so as not to lose him in the pitch black. He sniffed his nose and made a face no one could see. The air was getting more and more stale the deeper they walked into the abandoned lab. They had been through several doors and down not a few hallways as Joe led them through the labyrinth.

"None of this feels familiar, Joe," Donovan said, his voice mildly echoing in the halls. "The bunker door, sure, but not this place. You sure we're in the right spot?"

"Get power. Then we'll s-see," Joe said, a hint of frustration in his voice. Donovan shook his head, knowing Joe couldn't see the gesture but it still felt odd. He was getting tired of being led around with no real answers. He still didn't know how his wife was if she was alive at all, and they didn't seem to be closer to anything that explained what happening to him.

Donovan started to open his mouth to protest again when Joe suddenly let out a cry.

"Found it!"

Donovan jumped and clutched his chest, but moved forward to see what it was that Joe had found. There before them were several large metal cabinets with steel grated doors. Behind the doors were electrical panels, large fuses and switches.

"Great. Let's get the power on then," Donovan said as he opened one of the doors. "Joe, shine that little light over here."

"You can do it now," Joe answered.

"Yeah, shine some light and I'll get the breakers flipped on."

"No, p-p-power. Generators need boosted."

"Right, we just need to get these back… wait, what generators?"

Joe held the lighter toward the far cabinet, and Donovan opened to see three large generators stacked on top of one another. He turned to look at Joe, who looked expectantly back.

"Let me guess, I need to drum up some hidden power that I've had all along because it was my specialty?" Donovan said with a raised eyebrow. Joe merely smiled back. "I have no idea what you think I can do this time, Joe."

Joe sighed.

"You were the b-best. No one else could do what you could do. We t-t-tried. They stuck needles in us. Shocked us. Lit us on f-f-fire."

"That's what this place is, isn't it?" Donovan frowned. "They experimented on people here." Joe nodded. "Obviously it was shut down for a reason. And here we are firing everything back up."

"To remember," Joe said sternly. "So you can r-r-ember and get them back. And stop the b-bad ones."

"Like the bad lady?"

"Like the bad lady." Joe pointed to the cabinet again. "We need power. So you can remember." Donovan shook his head, then nodded and opened the far cabinet. He placed his hands flat against the generators and sighed.

"Okay, here goes nothing."

———————————

"Get me everything the city has on this precinct!" Bradley barked. "I want to see every floor plan, electrical, plumbing, everything as far back as you can find."

Three officers looked at each other then back at Bradley.

"Now!" He shouted. The three bolted from their position and headed for the elevators. Bradley shook his head and pulled out his phone. "Come on answer," he grumbled. The voicemail picked up again and he sighed. "Miller, you better not be dead. Call me back. I need to know what you've found out!" He closed his phone and marched into his office, slamming the door behind him. No sooner did he collapse into his chair, than his cell phone rang, and without looking he picked it up and shouted.

"Miller! About time you got back to me! Where are you?!"

"You should be more concerned with yourself right now, Lieutenant Bradley," came the cold voice on the other end. "You've stumbled into something you weren't supposed to know about, and it's just a matter of time before that mistake is rectified."

"Who is this?!" Bradley barked, then looked down at his phone to see the caller ID read *Unknown*.

"That's not important, you need to listen to me," the voice said.

"No, you need to tell me who this is and how you got my personal cell number. I've had enough with this clandestine bullshit!"

"They're coming, and if you don't do as I say you're not going to survive. If not for yourself, listen to me for those in your command."

Bradley grit his teeth, closed his eyes, and willed himself not to have an aneurysm. He took a deep breath and let it out through his teeth.

"Tell me what you know," he said in more of a grunt than actual words.

"This war is going to come back to your front doorstep. You need to evacuate that precinct while you still can, and take every weapon you have with you," the voice said.

"No can do. We're not leaving. Now it's your turn to tell me who you are and how you got this number," Bradley demanded.

"Don't say I didn't warn you." The call ended suddenly, leaving Bradley glaring at his phone. He tried to redial but there was no number to call back.

"Damnit!" He yelled as he tossed his phone on his desk. It immediately rang again.

"Listen you sonovabitch, you tell me what I want to know or so help me God I will find you, and when I do, you'll be—"

"Bradley! It's Agent Miller. I just got your messages," Miller said, as he cut off the lieutenant. "Meredith is insane, and she's one of them. She tried to kill me, she makes fire out of her hand. This is a nightmare we're dealing with here."

"Miller! Where are you? Did you reach O'Connell?"

"No, we didn't. That bitch pushed me out of the helicopter. I'm surprised I'm still alive. I'm headed to a Federal safe house. Tell me you've got something we can work with."

"I met with O'Connell's wife. She's still alive, and she's terrified. She brought up some big whig named Jonah who ran this whole thing. Where were you headed before Meredith tried to oust you?"

"She was certain they went to White Sands, New Mexico. Other than an Air Force base and proving grounds I don't know what else is there."

Bradley shook his head, even though Miller couldn't possibly see. "Follow that up if you can. I have a lead that this precinct might be under attack, among other things. Any of your Fed boys heading to White Sands?"

"Not yet, but I'll be sending as many as I can gather once I'm safe. Did you get Parker to talk?" Miller asked.

"I did. I'll tell you all about it when I see you next. Hurry. We're against the clock here." Bradley hung up the phone and shoved it in his pocket. So much for a quiet moment to himself.

Chapter 11
A Light for all Mankind

Sweat dripped down Donovan's forehead as he grunted and groaned and tried to summon whatever it was Joe thought he could do. The flame from the lighter had long since burnt out, and the two stood in utter darkness next to the generators. At least Donovan thought Joe was still there.

"Joe? You still there?" He asked. Joe grunted as the only response. "Look, I don't know what you expect to happen here, but maybe we can find another way. This just isn't working."

"You t-taught me," Joe muttered.

"I get that, but I don't know what you want me to do here. Nothing magical is happening. There has to be something else we can do."

"No, you taught me," Joe said again, his voice slightly different. A different pitch. A different way of saying the words. Something Donovan couldn't put a finger on but it was definitely something strange.

"How about you do it? Huh? I've been doing everything here and I don't even know where we are or what I'm looking for or what I'm supposed to be other than some enigmatic *general* that you say had all these specialties, and every damn time I try to use them my head feels like it's splitting open…" Donovan took a deep breath.

"No! You taught me!" Joe shouted into the darkness.

"I taught you what?!" Donovan turned from the generators and shouted back.

"You taught me! You wanted this!" The stutter was gone, Joe's voice echoed in the laboratory.

"I wanted what?! I didn't want this! I didn't want to be powerful, I wanted a normal life! You're the one leading me down this path, Joe!"

"You! You! You!" Joe repeated.

"I'm done with this! I'm done with these games!" Donovan turned back towards the generators and slammed his palms against the first one. The generator coughed and sputtered and roared to life. Small colored lights appeared on one of the electrical panels, and Donovan gawked in the near darkness.

"What the…" He stepped to the panel and reached for a breaker. A thin, blue hair of electricity popped out of the breaker and connected with his finger. He expected a shock, but nothing happened. The little blue connection danced and jerked side to side until Donovan pulled his finger back too far and the connection broke.

The moment he did, the lights flickered, and then died. Confused, he turned around to find Joe inches from his face.

"You need to start the others," he said, completely monotone and calm.

"How? What did I do?"

"Power."

Donovan sighed and marched to the other three generators. He hit his palms against the second one with a thud, but nothing happened.

"Power," Joe repeated, from somewhere behind him.

"You mean electricity?" Donovan asked. Joe didn't respond, so Donovan cursed under his breath and tried again.

Nothing.

"This is—" as he pulled his hands away, another little thin electric hair snaked out and danced it's jerky dance between Donovan's hand and the generator. "Wait a minute."

Donovan pressed his palms to his shirt and began rubbing up and down his chest rapidly. He could feel the fibers sticking to each other, and for a moment swore he could *feel* the static moving through his fingers.

"Ha. Haha. Hahaha!" Donovan laughed in excitement, pulled his hands away and watched hundreds of tiny blue worms crawling all over his hands. No, not just all over, but *in* his hands too. He carefully pressed his palms together, then held them forwards in a prayer position.

The tiny blue worms became a larger blue snake, that jumped in an instant from his fingertips to the second generator. It roared to life.

"Ha!" Donovan shouted, as he directed the electric snake to the third generator, reviving it from it's slumber as well. All the electrical panels lit up like Christmas, and Donovan broke the electric connection, and hurried to the panels. He flipped each breaker as fast as he could until the laboratory lit up, mostly, temporarily blinding him.

"I did it! I freaking did it!" Donovan cheered, turning to see Joe, who was facing away from him, staring at something else. "Joe! I did it!" Donovan's smile faded as his eyes found what Joe was looking at. Joy was replaced with terror as Donovan's gaze fell on the walls around them.

The floor.

The walls.

The ceiling, were scorched black with burn marks, and stained with splashes of deep red blood.

_____

Kathy took a sip of her water and sat back into her pillow, then let out a pained sigh. Her eye, or what was left of it she feared, had finally stopped aching. It might be healing, or maybe it was the slow, steady pumping of morphine into her veins. She turned her head to the side and looked lazily at the large machine next to her bed. It monitored her pulse, her oxygen levels, her brain function, and distributed that wonderful, pain soothing medicine she was so happy to have.

It wasn't like the old, traditional setup of a heart monitor and tubes and tanks and everything so cumbersome. Just a large automated machine with tubes plugged into the wall directly. Everything from oxygen, to antibiotics to morphine came from a much larger tank somewhere in the hospital. The machine merely monitored remotely and regulated the distribution of whatever was needed.

Kathy found solace in the simplicity and at the same time, complexity of the technology that kept her at ease and healing. Her mind wandered to days gone by, where such machines, or rather far more advanced machines, monitored the experiments she herself had once been a part of.

She shuddered. While she enjoyed the results of such experiments, the memory of how she got them was not at all a pleasant one. She remembered looking up through the glass dome of her capsule and seeing Donovan for the first time. Even in her semi-sedated state, she could tell just how handsome he was.

It was he who had personally worked with her, developing her meager skills in matter manipulation. It was hard for her not to blush and stutter and fumble through her training when Donovan was there. She was especially surprised, though delighted, when he invited her to be his personal assistant. She knew even then that it was largely because her skills hadn't developed as much as some of the other subjects. She knew it was pity for her weak progress that made him do it. While others, like Pyotr, were moving cars, she was lifting coins. Paperclips.

Bullets.

But the General liked her just the same, and worked with her privately when the two were alone. The relationship had never budded more than just purely platonic, at least not for the General. But for Kathy, Donovan was her knight in shining armor.

Then Jonah came, and ruined everything.

Kathy grimaced at just the thought of it. Life had been going so well until Jonah. It was his fault she was to be terminated from the program. He was the one that made the call that all weaker "subjects" should be discarded to make room for newer volunteers who showed better potential. If not for the General, she and several others would have simply been, eliminated. He literally saved her life. She knew then and there that he felt more for her than just that of another professional or coworker or colleague.

She took another sip of her water and cleared her now parched throat. Yes, there were times when she had wished it had been *her* memory that was wiped, and not Donovan's. Sure, everything turned up roses for her in the end, since she got to marry him and finally be his wife like she had fantasized about. But at what cost? She had to hide her abilities, and he his, and she was in constant fear that one day he would remember everything, and her fairy tale would end.

And actually, it did. The look on his face when everything went to hell at the casino still haunted her. She didn't care about the other guests, she didn't care about the chaos or the carnage. She had seen all that before as part of the program. No, it was the look in his eyes that terrified her. In that moment, Donovan didn't look like Donovan. He looked like *him.*

She was startled as her room phone suddenly rang. The heart monitor came alive, registering the quickened pace of her pulse.

"Hello? My phone is ringing," she called out to the officer posted outside her hospital room door. "Hello?" No answer. She could see the silhouette of the officer, but obviously he didn't hear her. The phone kept ringing. Kathy grumbled and reached over as best she could, stretching her arm out but it was just out of reach. She grunted and focused and tried to steady her breathing.

Just like he had taught her.

At last the receiver lifted from the base and gently floated into her outstretched hand as though someone had passed it to her.

"Hello?"

"What did you tell them?" The man's voice said, in a cold and frustrated tone. Kathy's heart stopped and her ears began to ring.

"I…I didn't tell them a thing," she lied.

"You're lying, Kathy. I could always tell when you're lying, you know," the man said. "Tell me what you told them. It's imperative to O'Connell's survival."

"Please," Kathy squeaked, her voice breaking.

"Tell me what you told the authorities about O'Connell," the man said, more demanding.

"You know more than I do. Just, leave him alone for once will you? Please, Jonah," Kathy swallowed hard, as a tear rolled down her cheek.

"I cannot help… Donovan, unless I know what the authorities know." His voice shifted, softer, gentler, but still with a cold emptiness behind it.

Kathy took a deep breath and closed her eyes. She knew she was out of her depth here, and maybe he was right anyway. Maybe he was the only one who could keep Donovan alive.

And bring him back to her.

"I told the Lieutenant what I knew about the casino."

"Everything?"

"Enough. But not everything."

"I need specifics. What *else* did you tell him?"

"I told him… I uh, about Siobhan, about Donovan, about…" she hesitated and closed her eyes tight. "I told him about Blindsight."

Silence.

Kathy listened to her own unsteady breathing for what seemed like an eternity.

"Good. Thank you. I'm doing everything I can for Donovan, but it's going to take everyone to fix this," the man she identified as Jonah finally answered. Kathy let out a shaky breath.

"Siobhan is in the field," she blurted out. "She's not dead after all."

More silence.

"I didn't know that," he broke the silence. "Thank you, Kathy, you have been a big help."

The call ended, and Kathy slowly floated the receiver back onto the base of the phone, then closed her eyes and tried to steady her breathing. Next to her bed, the readouts on the machine started to change. Some numbers slowly began to climb, higher and higher, one digit at a time, while another began to drop at the same rate. Kathy let out another sigh, but this one more relaxed. Her head sank into her pillow deeper, as she was finally able to relax more than she had in days. Weeks. Her whole life.

Her one good eye opened wider, and she rolled her head lazily to one side to look at the machine. She saw the numbers, she even understood what they meant, but her mind was quickly losing the battle of drowsiness. Too much morphine was pumping into her veins. Too much oxygen was cutting off. The machine's life support was being overridden.

Kathy closed her eye, and imagined Donovan one last time. She smiled, and the heart monitor alert sounded.

Then suddenly the entire machine just switched off.

Donovan's heart pounded in his chest as he stepped warily from horror scene to horror scene. The grey concrete walls and silver metal siding that would seem so sterile were either blackened and burnt, or painted red with dried blood.

Or both.

To say that carnage had taken place here was an understatement, and Donovan was mortified with each step. He swallowed hard as he and Joe moved from the electrical room, to the open space from before, and into a room called "Incubation". He didn't understand any of it, and he wasn't sure he really wanted to.

"Joe," he quietly muttered, "what happened here?"

"Big fight," Joe replied dryly. "B-b-bad lady. General. Big fight."

"You mean *I* did this?!" Donovan was taken aback at the accusation.

"No. Yes. Some of it," Joe shrugged.

Donovan shook his head as they came upon large beds with domed glass coverings, some broken, that acted as lids of sorts over the beds. Frayed wires and busted control panels connected to each bed, some completely destroyed, marked an uneasy scene where human experiments had taken place. He looked at the dozen beds, six on each side of the room, and buried his head in his hands.

Then he noticed something on the wall. He moved closer next to a picture with writing on the bottom, a Polaroid with a man and woman. Peering at the semi-burnt photo he gasped. There he clearly was, in Marine Corp fatigues, next to a redheaded woman in blue scrubs, her arm around his waist and huge smile on her face. Written below were the scorched words...

A light for all mankind

Donovan's jaw dropped when he noticed the woman's other hand was completely engulfed in flames.

"Joe, tell me who this woman is," he said, his voice hoarse.

"Bad lady," Joe muttered.

"General!" Came a woman's voice, echoed in the laboratory. "General, I know you're here!" She screeched.

"Who the hell is that?" Donovan whispered. Joe thrust a fat finger at the picture.

"Bad... lady..."

Chapter 12
Lover's Spat

"Sir, you need to see this," said a female officer as she poked her head into Lieutenant Bradley's office. He groaned as he got up and marched around his desk towards the door.

"What is it?"

"What you asked us to look into. We found something you really need to see," she said, as she started for the elevator.

"Can't you just tell me? I'm in the middle of something important," Bradley grumbled.

"That's just it, sir. We're not sure what we're looking at. Not really."

Bradley raised an eyebrow, but thought it best not to ask anymore questions until they got to where they were going. The officer hit the basement button on the elevator, and they rode in silence down several floors until they came to the basement. Once the door opened, Bradley followed her into a large space with empty grey walls and neutral lighting that would make you sick if you spent too much time under them.

The other two officers Bradley had put on the task were down there as well, and several large metal racks, and not a few boxes had been cleared away from an empty wall. Bradley approached and looked it over, then turned to the female officer.

"Well? Someone want to tell me what I'm looking at here?" He said, his patience wearing thin.

"This wall," one of the other officers began, "shouldn't be here. I mean it should but it's not in the original plans. We found the old, *old* plans for this precinct. This basement is too small, and everything points to the wall here being added around eighty years ago." He beamed proudly as though expecting a treat or a pat on the head.

Bradley moved forward and touched the wall gingerly, feeling the old drywall and cracked paint on the wall.

"Fifty," he said, as he turned to look at the officers. "Drywall replaced most interior walls in the 1970s, so it would be around fifty years ago. Still…" he tapped on several places on the wall, each producing a dull sound. "Hmm."

Bradley sighed.

He walked to a maintenance locker and perused through a minute before coming back with a small sledge hammer in hand. With a deep breath, he swung and struck hard against the drywall. It dented but did not break through. He struck again, and then again. The drywall cracked everywhere but didn't bust through. He struck once more, knocking a swath about a square foot in size off, revealing old red brick behind the drywall.

"Hmmm," he grunted again.

"Nothing?" The third officer asked.

"No. Not nothing. These old basement walls were poured concrete. *Not* red brick." Bradley grinned and swung again. He struck the brick, sending chips flying. Then again. And again. And again, until one of the bricks broke through and fell off into the other side. A waft of stale air poured into the basement, hitting Bradley square in the face, and causing the other officers to back away. Bradley bent down and peered through the newly made hole and scoffed.

"You three get to work," he said as he tossed the hammer to one of the men. "Let me know when you clear enough to walk through." With that, he left them to their work. "I'll be damned," he muttered to himself as he headed back to the elevator. Parker had been right, there *was* something under the precinct after all. Now he just needed to find out what.

"Why don't you come out and chat, General?" Meredith taunted. "It's been years, don't you want to see me?"

Donovan crouched behind a wall in one of the offices, but he dare not turn off the light and attract too much attention. He looked over to Joe, who sat huddled in a corner in the same office, a bewildered look on his face.

"Joe. Psst, Joe!" Donovan whispered. "Who is this woman?"

"Bad lady," Joe repeated.

"Yeah I gathered that. But *who* is she?"

"You need to f-f-fight her. We need to l-leave," Joe said, as he began to rock back and forth.

"Is there another way out?" Joe shook his head frantically. "Shit."

"General! Come out come out! You can't hide from me forever!" Meredith's voice was followed by the telltale noise of rushing flames. Donovan could swear he felt the air around him heat and Joe clenched his eyes shut tight as it did.

"Joe, help me out. What do I do?"

"Go fight," Joe urged.

"How? Fight how?"

"Use your s-specialties," Joe demanded.

"And do what exactly!?"

Joe shook his head and sighed, then closed his eyes and threw his head back.

"Siobhan you crazy psycho!" Donovan's eyes shot wide open as Joe shouted. Joe looked down directly into Donovan's eyes with a smug smile. "There, now go fight."

"Joe? Well this is a surprise," Meredith announced. "Why don't you come out and play?"

"Dammit, Joe!" Donovan hissed. He took a few sharp breaths and got to his feet, then cautiously made his way out of the open office door. He looked left and right around every corner until he came to the main room and saw her standing there, her red hair tied up in a beehive, thick rimmed glasses on, wearing a full business pinstripe dress.

"There you are," she smiled.

"Look, I don't know who you are, or what you want with me, but maybe we can come to some sort of arrangement?"

Meredith smirked.

"You really don't remember anything, do you?"

"That's what I'm trying to tell you. Whatever history you and I may have had, I don't have the foggiest clue. So let's solve this without violence, and maybe we can help each other," Donovan swallowed hard. Meredith squinted her eyes to measure up Donovan then shrugged.

"Where's Joe?"

"Let's just solve this, you and me, and leave him out of it, yes?"

Meredith shook her head. "No deal. Bring him out and maybe you and I can talk."

"That's not going to happen," Donovan said, firmly.

"I was kind of hoping you'd say that, General," she grinned, and her eyes lit up with fire.

The next few moments were a blur for Donovan. The air around him got hot, hotter than anything he had ever felt, and it was as if everything combusted at once. His fists hit his forehead, and his elbows smashed together hard, sending out a disgustingly painful loud noise of bones crashing, covering his face like a shield. Everything around him was hot, searingly painful, like he had just been thrust into Hell. But when he opened his eyes, the fire was *around* him, not burning him.

In fact, other than the intense heat, he was otherwise completely unharmed. A few moments passed by and the flames died down, leaving a stinking smell of burning in the air. There was acrid smoke, but even that cleared within seconds. Donovan looked up through his arms to see Meredith gawking in surprise.

"And here I thought you would just roll over and die," she said as she chuckled. "This'll be fun after all."

Donovan stood to his feet, defiantly, and faced her.

"You can tell me who you are, and what you want, or I can—"

"You can what? Huh? Make me? Stop me? Couldn't do any of that before, what makes you think you can now?" Meredith scoffed. "Where's Joe?"

"What's your name?"

"Where's Joe?"

"Tell me, your name," two office chairs far off to the side slowly righted themselves.

"You bring Joe out here, and I'll tell you my name."

"Nope. It's not going to work that way," Donovan said, as he lowered his head and glared through his eyelashes at Meredith. The two chairs slowly lifted off the ground.

"Four years, *four* years I thought you were dead. We all did," Meredith took a step closer.

The chairs hovered a foot off the ground.

"Four years! Not one word from you. And after everything we'd been through, you resurface and what, you're *married* to that talentless skank?!" Meredith took another step, the chairs turned so the cushioned side faced her.

"Don't… refer to my wife… that way," Donovan growled. "You're beef is with me, whatever it is."

"What *ever* it is?! Are you seriously telling me you don't know who I am?!" Meredith was now advancing on Donovan. His right and left hands both jerked towards his thighs, and the chairs lunged through the air, coming together to fit like puzzle pieces around Meredith, locking her arms to her sides and lifting her a few inches off the ground.

"You're kidding with this, right?" She screamed and threw her head back, and the chairs burst into flames. The cushions burnt to ash in moments, and the frames of the chairs melted into useless, molten pools of stinking charred plastic on the floor. Donovan's eyes shot open wide as he watch his little trap fail. Meredith's heels clacked on the floor as she came back down, and she thrust her hands out in front of her, sending a torrent of flame cascading towards Donovan's head.

He held up his hands and howled as they ignited with the flames, and he swung them to the side trying to put the fire out, but instead threw the flames themselves against one of the concrete walls, making new scorch marks. He looked at the burnt wall a moment and turned towards Meredith.

"You," he muttered. "You did this. You killed these people. You wrecked this place," he looked around in astonishment. "I was here, too. But, I didn't… I don't do…this."

"Oh come off it, General. Everything that happened to all of us is your fault. *You* recruited me! You trained me! You loved me! Then you abandoned me! All of us! Everything that happened is your fault," Meredith pulled her arms back and thrust forward as though to shove Donovan from a distance, but fire soared out instead.

Donovan held up his hands, catching the flames without burning himself this time. The pain seared through the back of his skull and his vision blurred, but he gritted his teeth and shook his head.

"No," he growled through the pain. "I'm not a monster. You are." His vision shifted, the world around him turned a light blue, and little blue worms crawled in his veins. He clapped his hands together, and a flash of blue light pulsed through the air, struck Meredith and sent her convulsing to the ground. The fire died and sparks flew all around him as the lights brightened, flickered, and a dozen bulbs in various rooms popped.

Meredith stopped convulsing and rolled to her face, pushing herself up onto her knees. Donovan looked triumphantly down at her from a few feet away.

"Had enough?"

Her face rose and her gaze met his.

She was laughing.

"I missed you so much," she said through a disturbing smile.

"Agh!" Donovan shouted as he was thrust straight into the air by a massive fireball. His clothes singed as his back struck the ceiling three stories up. Gravity claimed him next, and he began to fall thirty feet to the hard floor below, when his momentum was suspended a few inches from the ground, then dropped onto his face.

Joe was standing in the doorway, a hand held out, fingers stretched out. Donovan, tried to catch his breath, his face to the floor, and he heard a low rumble of Joe's voice.

Page 141

"You disgust me, Siobhan. You always did," he heard Joe say.

"Joe? There you are," she cooed.

"You're pathetic. No wonder Donovan chose Kathy over you," Joe taunted.

"You don't mean that," Meredith growled through gritted teeth. "You love me. Not her. Admit it!" She screeched. Donovan heard the sound of roaring flames and he thought it might be nice to just close his eyes and accept that this was his fate. His body rose from the floor, eyes still closed, chin down, though he was anything but unconscious.

The fire roared.

Heat surrounded him. But once again it didn't consume him. He felt the flames, the air burn, oxygen being consumed in the large open room. His jaw set.

The air crackled.

The floor under his feet quaked.

There was crashing and banging, metal and concrete, in a sickening sound that threatened to shatter his eardrums. Then came the all too familiar sensation of flying, as his body launched backwards.

Back and back and back, as brick and metal and rock made way just for him. Through walls that would take a wrecking ball to clear, he punched through like they were Japanese paper doors. He crashed through glass and landed hard against a soft, fluffy surface. The air crackled again and lights came alive, just for him. When he opened his eyes he was sitting on a cushioned bench in a train car. He looked over and saw Joe laying on the floor, cut and bruised and out cold.

"Huh," he grunted. He looked up and saw hole after hole in wall after wall. Then he saw Meredith standing in the far most opening, almost a lifetime away. Just a small figure, yet he saw her cut lip, a trail of blood on her forehead, and her dress ripped in multiple places. She was far from ugly. She screamed something at him he couldn't hear.

A quick survey of his new environment told him he was in some sort of underground train station, probably part of the lab, he assumed. Donovan turned his head towards what he thought was the front of the train and waved as though trying to tell someone to move. The train lurched forward, the engines came alive, and the train car started down a dark tunnel on a strange track.

"Joe," he mumbled. "We need to have a talk, buddy."

Then he passed out.

Chapter 13
Light at the End of the Tunnel

Agent Miller asked for fifteen agents to accompany him. Five analysts, and ten field agents. He had seen more than enough to know that he would need all the help he could get if he were to confront Meredith, O'Connell, or God knows who else.

The Bureau sent him five analysts, and that was it.

What the hell are they thinking?!

Chances are, they weren't. But when he called to complain, all he got was the runaround, and some excuse about a recently discovered terror plot on six U.S. cities all at once, and that every available field agent was being reassigned. The timing couldn't be worse for Miller, and likely, he thought, was no coincidence either.

Still, he had to make due with what he had. He had asked one of the analysts when the last time he had been to the range and discharged his firearm. The answer was less than encouraging for Miller.

"Uh, not since Academy," the agent had said. Miller smiled and patted him on the shoulder, and cursed the Bureau.

"We leave in five minutes," Miller said to his new team. "We'll head back to Las Vegas and give Lieutenant Bradley some assistance. I'm sure he'll be grateful for it." Without trained field agents, Miller didn't want to run into Meredith again, who apparently controlled fire. This whole situation was getting weirder and weirder by the hour, and he figured the analysts might be able to shed some new light on anything the LVPD had found.

Then the hardline phone rang.

Miller spun fast on his heels and looked at the phone in shock. No one should know about that line, and his point of contact at the Bureau knew they were heading out as soon as the team arrived. He reluctantly reached for the handset.

"Agent Miller," he said as sternly as he could.

"Get a pen and write this down," came a man's voice. It was the same voice from earlier.

"How do you have *this* number?"

"Agent Miller, I'm trying to help you, but we're running out of time. Get. A. Pen."

Miller paused and sighed, then pulled open a drawer on the desk and began rustling through.

"Hold on, hold on," he murmured, holding the handset between his jaw and shoulder as he rummaged with both hands now. "Got it. What's the phone number?"

"It's not a phone number. They're coordinates. You need to go to these coordinates."

"Coordinates? Why?"

"This is the last known location for O'Connell, and the woman you know as Meredith Brown. Follow these and get inside. Once there, I can guide you."

"Wait, how do you know all this?" Miller interjected. There was silence, then a strained sigh.

"Trust me, or don't. O'Connell needs to be stopped, and if you can't do it, I'll find someone else," the man said.

"Just give me the coordinates," Miller shook his head as the voice slowly listed each number. "Ok, ok, I got it. Can you at least tell me your name?"

"Once you reach that location, I'll contact you again. Then I'll tell you everything. This line isn't secure."

Miller knew that was a lie. Every line the Bureau used was secure. He furrowed his eyebrows as something else didn't make sense.

"This line isn't secure?" He said out loud. "Who says that?" He looked at the phone, as if the phone had all the answers. With a sigh and a shrug he figured he might as well play along, since this was about the only lead he had, anymore.

The call ended. Miller slowly put down the handset and looked over the coordinates. He shook his head and walked out of the small office to where his team was waiting.

"Change of plans, everyone."

Bradley stood unmoving with his hands on his hips, as his eyes slowly panned left to right at the scene before him. It wasn't often that he was surprised, except lately anyway. But as his mind reeled at the implications of what he was looking at, he felt more surprised than he had, at least in the last twenty-four hours. Voices gently swirled in the air around his confused head, making their way into his ears, but only barely. His ears were ringing for whatever reason, and that ringing overtook the voices that calmly, if not worriedly, vied for his attention at the moment.

"Lieu…"

"…ley…"

"…okay?"

"Lieutenant?"

"…Bradley, are you okay?"

He blinked out of his stupor and turned his eyes to the three officers that were looking at him, rather concerned, as they all stood in the damp, dimly lit, vast red brick cavern. His nostrils flared as the scent of stale air and mold crept into his nose. He'd smelled that pungent fragrance before, though he couldn't place it at the moment.

"Huh? Yes… yes I'm fine," Bradley cleared his throat and nodded. "I'm fine."

"What do you make of this, sir?" Asked the female officer, after giving a quick glance to her companions.

This, she was referring to, was the large stone staircase that descended from the false wall in the basement of the LVPD, and the huge opening the staircase led to. Bradley gazed around at the damp red brick, the wooden bookcases, mostly broken, scattered around the floor. The dust-filled shelves on the walls, and most disconcerting, the large cylindrical glass and metal tanks that lined a wall in a room with a thick glass window.

It was a lot to take in.

"We've been played for fools, that's what I think. Get someone from forensics down here," Bradley muttered. "No wait," he paused as one of the officers started up the stairs. "Get two from forensics down here. Don't tell anyone else about it, though. Be discrete," he said to the officer, who nodded his understanding and headed up the stairs.

"What do we do, Lieutenant?" The female officer asked.

"First we figure out what the hell was going on down here. Whatever this is," he waved a hand around the place, as his eyes fell on something in the dim distance. "Hand me your light," he said to the male officer, as he held out a hand. The second officer handed over his long flashlight and Bradley shined it into the distance. His eyes squinted as he spotted what he caught a glimpse of.

"Next, we find out where that train track goes to, and where it comes from," he said as the other officers gazed out at the two opposite tunnels, and the singular track that ran between them. "I want to know everything. Get on it," Bradley growled. He stepped down from the last step and slowly walked to the edge of a platform that overlooked the track. He sniffed the air.

"Fresh air," he said to no one. "Is this thing active?"

Donovan sat on a train car bench alone, having left Joe passed out on the floor of another car. He had made his way two cars up and sat, lost in his thoughts as the train sped along near silent. He twisted his wedding band slowly on his finger, as Kathy entered his mind. It had been days since the casino incident, but it felt like a lifetime ago. Kathy felt like a distant memory.

He hadn't really had a moment to himself to just sit and ponder everything that had taken place. One day he was a normal man living a normal life, and the next his whole world was turned on it's head and he was on the run from the law and for his life. It didn't seem fair, he liked the way things were, and yet something in him also liked the things that were happening to him. Something in him liked the power.

He shook his head.

No, he was a freak now, plagued with unnatural abilities that ostracized him from the rest of the world. Cursed by whatever was happening to him now, whatever he was becoming. Or whatever he *was* beforehand. He didn't want to know anything more about who he apparently had been, he was happy with who he was. But each time he discovered, or *re-discovered* another one of his so called "specialties", he felt a rush inside his chest. It made him feel... strong.

When his head wasn't splitting open, that was. He reached back and massaged the base of his skull, where the pain always began every time he used one of his newfound powers. It had gotten to the point where he almost always felt like passing out, and sometimes he did. He rubbed the spot, massaging the muscles in his neck.

Then he felt it. Something small, something hard. He concentrated on the spot in his upper neck, near the brain stem, and could definitely feel something. Almost like a grain of rice, lodged just under the skin. He pressed on it and the pain shot through him like someone had just hit his skull with a hammer. It burned, it made his eyes roll back, and he willed himself not to pass out.

"No... ugh... not this... time... argh!" He grunted, gritted his teeth and fought the urge to vomit. His heart raced and sweat beaded on his forehead.

"What is that?" He said to the floor.

He reached back again, gentler this time, and touched it with the tip of his finger. He closed his eyes tight, one had over his mouth, and concentrated, slowly raising his finger from his flesh and willing the thing to come out. It tugged gently on his skin, like a pimple begging to be popped. But it wouldn't be removed.

Donavan jumped to his feet and ran down the train cars until he came to where Joe was still sleeping on the floor. There was shattered glass everywhere where he and Joe had burst into the train car earlier. He seized a piece of sharp glass and carefully felt around the back of his neck with it. He gingerly cut a small line in the skin.

"Careful now," he said to himself. "Let's not kill ourselves, shall we?" He gently tapped his forefinger against the new cut, as though tugging on a fishing line when the fish were so close to taking a bite. The thing in his neck edged closer and closer, pulled by an invisible string.

The pain in his head began to swell.

"No you don't," he said, furrowing his eyebrows. He tugged a little more, and could feel the foreign object squelching through the muscles and blood towards his finger. He closed his eyes tight, as the more he used his ability, the more his head hurt, like a migraine pulsing through his skull.

Then the thing flew out and made contact with the tip of his finger. The headache immediately ceased. He gasped in relief and took a few deep breaths, then Donovan gently moved his hand around to see what was causing the pain, expecting a small tumor, a rock, even a bullet fragment for all he knew. He stared down at the thing, no bigger than a TicTac.

It was mechanical in nature, a clear casing that housed tiny circuitry. He looked closely at it, as close as his eyes would allow him to focus. And there it was on the tiny little device, the crosshair symbol of Blindsight. His eyes went wide.

As he looked up into the reflection of the glass across from him, as the train sped along a dark track, he saw two nurses standing by a bedside in the glass, like watching a scene on a dimly lit television screen. There was a doctor in a long white lab coat pulling a sheet over a woman's face.

It was Kathy.

The scene faded from view as the black tunnel outside the train began to give way to light. Soft at first, the light soon seemed to illuminate the entire tunnel as the train slowed down. A single tear fell from Donovan's eye while his jaw twitched but no words came out. It seemed so real, so vivid, like the trickle of blood crawling down his neck. He looked to the floor just in time to see Joe sit up like a man waking from the dead.

"Oh," he said with a smile. "W-w-we're here."

———————————

Agent Miller exited the rattling elevator and stepped into the burnt and broken laboratory, deep beneath White Sands. Most the lights were on, while some flickered and others were very broken. He looked left to right and sighed.

"All right, get to work. Let's see what we can make of this place," He said to his crew of analysts, who were all too eager to see something new and exciting. The place had seen better days, and there was a lingering smell of sulfur in the air. Miller was too acquainted with the acrid scent, after smelling it on his charred shirt and tie.

"There's power, and the computers are active," one of there analysts said. "But… the systems are down. We might be able to reboot them. We'll just have to cycle the power."

"Do it. Then find out what you can from those computers and let me know. I want everything on what this place was, what they did here, and how O'Connell is involved." Miller said as he looked around the place, shaking his head. He kicked at charred papers and bent over to inspect what looked like the melted armrest of a computer chair.

"What in the hell happened down here?" He muttered to himself as he stood and caught a glimpse of a hole in a wall. When he moved to a better angle he saw there was not one, but multiple holes through multiple walls leading all the way back into darkness. "What the hell happened down here?" His voice carried as he asked aloud.

After a few minutes, the lights died, leaving only red emergency lights on, then the power came back on with a loud *whooshing* sound.

"That should do it," the analyst said. Instantly the phone on a console rang. Miller snatched it up and held it to his ear.

"Hello?"

"Good job, Agent Miller," the familiar voice said.

"Now do you want to tell me what's going on here? What is this place? Who are you?"

"One thing at a time," the man said. The analyst sat back in one of the chairs as he watched the screen light up with dozens of files appearing at once.

"Fine," Miller sighed, "how does all this relate to O'-Connell?"

"This is, or was, the White Sands Research Facility. As you can see it was decommissioned after the incident."

"What incident?"

"We'll get to that. For now, I need you to repair some damaged files so I can access them remotely."

"You're going to repair some damaged files so…" Miller began telling the analyst. "Wait a minute. I'm not helping you anymore until I know who I'm talking to."

Silence.

The analysts all looked at Agent Miller and they all waited patiently to see if there would be an answer.

"I'm the one in charge of Blindsight," the man finally said.

"Uh huh, give me a name or we're done here."

"You need me to decode the—"

"I'll figure out the rest with my team." Miller interrupted as he nodded to the five eager analysts. There was another long pause, then the line went dead.

Chapter 14
JONAH

Donovan slowly peeked his head out of the open train car door, with more caution than he probably should have. There hadn't been any signs of movement or sound since the train arrived ten minutes ago. He was certain there would be some guard, some cop, *someone* that would storm in any minute now and arrest him. But no one came.

"I think it's s-s-safe," Joe whispered.

"What's safe? Where the hell are we?" Donovan whispered back. "I can hardly make anything out."

"You need to go look," Joe said as he stood up from his crouched position next to Donovan and stepped out of the train.

"Joe! *Joe!*" Donovan cursed and stood and followed. A red laser appeared out from somewhere on the ceiling, fanned up and down over Donovan a few times. He froze still until the light died away. He looked left to right but no one appeared, no gun fired, no missile came to blow him up.

"We m-m-made it. Now you can remember!" Joe said excitedly as he turned to face Donovan.

"Where is everybody?" Donovan looked around the large domed room and began to take it all in. There was more than enough light, and a false ceiling gave the impression that there was a blue sky with puffy white clouds at least forty feet above their heads. He could see the track they came in on, that dead-ended at a large circular platform, and as they stood there the platform lowered to reveal a massive turntable.

"It's a… transit hub," Donovan whispered to himself. "But for what?"

"Trains, obviously," a woman's voice caught him off guard and he spun around to see a thin woman who hadn't seen the sun for a while, with platinum blonde hair, and large glasses. She wore a business pant suit, but tennis shoes instead of heels or even flats. She carried a computer tablet in one hand and a stylus in the other.

"And you are…" she checked her tablet and smiled. "Oh, General Erst. You haven't visited us for, it says, four years now. How can I help you, General?"

Donovan cleared his throat. He didn't recognize the name Erst, but this woman clearly knew who he was, or at least she seemed to.

"Um, well, my friend and I are looking for," Donovan cleared his throat, glanced at Joe who was busy looking around like a tourist in Manhattan. "Um, Blindsight."

The woman looked down to her tablet and tapped it a few times with the stylus.

"Hmm, Blindsight, Blindsight. Project Bell… Project Blue Book… Project, oh! Here it is, Blindsight. You'll be wanting to see Jonah, then," the woman smiled.

"Jonah," Donovan repeated. I'm sorry Ms.?"

"Jennifer!" The woman beamed.

"Jennifer, right. It's been four years," Donovan feigned ignorance. "Since I haven't been back in a while, my memory is a little foggy. Could you point me in the direction where I might find, Jonah?"

"Of course," Jennifer spun around and pointed. "We're here at the Aurelion, so you'll want to head straight away towards the two inclinators. Take the one on your *right*, that's right from our current perspective, like stage right, not proper right, and go down to level," she checked her tablet, "oh, wow. Level B-5. So, all the way down."

Donovan smiled, though not much of her directions made sense. "Great, and just a refresher, where is all this again? Like, *all* this." He waved a hand around.

"You're at the Aurelion, General," Jennifer smiled, her eyes somewhat bulging in her thick glasses.

"Of course. The Auralon," he said. Jennifer chuckled.

"Au-re-li-on," she said, sounding out the syllables. "The Aurora-Echelon Unified Relay for Experimental Logistics, Intelligence & Operations Nexus. It's sometimes easier to remember it that way," she batted her eyes and grinned.

"Way easier," Donovan smacked his forehead with his palm, which made Jennifer chortle out loud.

"You're so much fun, General! I missed you. If you need anything else just holler, I'm always here! Well almost always. They let me out every once in a while. 'Don't go too far, Jen, we might need you'. 'You're contractually obligated to fulfill your term, Jen'. You know how it is," she gave a snort and Donovan was certain he made a face.

"Well, that's me off then. Thanks again, Jen!" He gave two thumbs up in a comic fashion and she replied in kind. Then he quickly strode off in the direction she had mentioned.

"Th-th-that was weird," Joe muttered.

"You're telling me. And she knew who I was."

"Biometric scan," Joe shrugged.

"Huh?"

"Big red laser. Scanned your f-f-face and all." Donovan's eyes went wide.

"Wait a minute, so someone knows we're here?"

Joe nodded. "She r-r-read your profile. She didn't care though, so I guess we're okay."

"Let's hope so. You said I'd remember once we got here, that we'd find answers here. That still the case?"

Joe nodded. "Inclinator," he pointed at two steal doors against a wall.

"Here goes nothing."

"Sir you have to see this!" One of the analysts shouted as Miller was reading through scores of notebooks. He nearly dropped the stack in his arms when the man shouted at him, but he could hardly blame him. There was an absolute treasure trove of information dating back decades on all kinds of experiments run at this facility alone. Miller was starting to appreciate the fact that the Bureau had only sent him analysts.

"What have we got?" He leaned over the chair of the man who called to him and looked at the screen.

"You won't believe the kinds of things that were done here. They were researching every myth on expanded mental states that I've ever heard of, and about a dozen I've never known about before in my life! It's so cool!" He looked at Agent Miller like a kid in a candy store with his parents' credit card.

"Good, good. What about anything on O'Connell?" Miller asked, as he tried to make sense of the data he was looking at.

"Nothing about him being experimented on here, but there's loads of files with," he scrolled through a few files until he found what he was looking for, "'The General', they called him, right?"

"Makes sense, he was a Marine Corp General," Miller shrugged. "Wait, what's that?" He pointed at a video file. "Can you access this one?"

"Probably," the analyst double clicked and the file came up. "Hmm, it looks like it's corrupted. Audio only."

"Play it anyway."

"Patient interview. Subject Jacob Orletta Erst." A man's voice said on the recording.

"General is fine," the second man's voice came over the recording next.

"Who's Jacob Erst?" Miller asked to no one as they all continued to listen to the recording.

"How are you feeling today, General?"

"Ready to be out of this chair. Is this really necessary?"

"Just standard procedure," the first man said. *"Tell me, have you been experiencing any dizziness? Fatigue? Light-headedness?"*

"Nothing out of the ordinary, doc. Only what you people said to expect."

There was the sound of something scraping across the floor, and the analyst looked up at Miller questioningly. Miller shook his head once, indicating he didn't know what that sound was, and he pointed to the screen.

"Keep listening."

"That. How did you do that?" The man identified as some sort of doctor asked.

"Oh, that? That's nothing. You want to see something really cool? Ask O'Connell."

"I'm asking you. *How did you move that chair?"*

"Like this," the General said, and there was another scraping noise, only slightly heavier sounding this time.

"Ok, that's enough," the doctor said. The General chuckled and the scraping sound happened again.

"*Let's be serious now, please. I, uh, that is have you ever, uh—*" more scraping.

"*What's the matter, doc? Isn't this what your lot does down here anyway?*" The scraping continued back and forth, while the doctor made more noises of protest and the General began to laugh with each new sound.

"*Security! Help! Someone please… restrain him!*" The doctor shouted. There was the sound of a door opening and footsteps, a struggle, the chair crashing onto the floor and the General laughing. Then the recording ended.

The analyst looked up at Miller with worried eyes, whereas before he had been more than excited.

"Sir, this isn't… real, is it?"

Miller swallowed hard and looked at the shocked faces of the other analysts who had been listening to the recording as well.

"See what else you can find," Miller finally said. "And try to fix the video feed on that. I want to know more about who the other guy in the room is. We might have more… enhanced to deal with."

The inclinator was exactly as it sounded, an elevator that rose and descended at an incline rather than straight up and down. Donovan and Joe rode in relative silence, save for Joe's humming some tune that Donovan couldn't quite place, though it sounded familiar. The inclinator was slow, and the distance was vast. They needed to reach the fifth sub-basement level, and each level was roughly fifty feet from floor to ceiling.

Donovan stared out a small window that didn't show much, just the concrete walls of the shaft outside their slow moving car. He didn't know *why* he was here, other than Joe's insistence that searching more would make him remember. And he shifted back and forth from wanting to remember and just wanting to get back to his normal life.

Though there wasn't much of a life to get back to. He was almost certain that Kathy was dead, if his vision could be believed, and he was still wanted for the death and injury of dozens of people, not to mention untold amounts of property damage. Going back to Las Vegas wasn't an option for him if he wanted any semblance of freedom.

The car suddenly slowed to a stop and the silver doors opened, revealing a long, dark hallway.

"Uhh," Donovan peered out of the open doors. "Does this look right to you, Joe?"

"I dunno," he muttered. "W-w-we have to go s-see." With that, Joe marched off into the darkness. A few steps in and lights came on, obviously triggered by some kind of motion sensor. There was nothing in the hall except for a single door at the very end, roughly fifty yards down.

"Yeah, this doesn't feel ominous at all," Donovan mused. "So we just go down and find this Jonah guy, and he's going to help me remember everything and then I can sort out what's happening. Got it," he said to Joe, but was certain Joe wasn't listening at all. Each step seemed to echo into eternity, and since Joe was no longer talking, all Donovan could hear were his own footsteps and the sound of his breathing. That, and the pounding heartbeat in his ears.

They both reached the door and stood still a moment.

"Well?" Joe asked. "Are you going in?"

"*We* are, yes. But... how?"

Joe smiled. "Use your specialty."

Donovan nodded, held out a hand and focused on the door with his eyes narrowed. "Open. Please?"

As if on cue, locks from the other side began loudly churning as though it had been a while since they were used. The door opened to near blinding light, the white room on the other side reflected lights from the ceiling and walls.

"Good day," a man's voice said.

―――――――

The phone rang, and Miller quickly snatched it up from beside the computer.

"Hello, who's this?" Miller asked, but somehow he already knew the answer to his question.

"Good day, Agent Miller, I'm glad you found what you were looking for."

―――――――

Donovan held a hand to his face and squinted, trying to see into the large white room. His eyes slowly adjusted as he and Joe stepped inside.

"Who are you? What is this place?" He asked, looking at the floor and slowly raising his eyes.

"This is the main operational center for Blindsight," the man said.

"And you are?" Donovan turned his eyes upward at the massive spherical machine before him. He furrowed his eyebrows in confusion as lights danced all over a giant metallic ball. The man's voice came from everywhere, and nowhere specific.

―――――――

"You want to tell me who you are now?" Miller asked.

"Of course," the man said.

_____

"Allow me to reintroduce myself, General. My name is Jonah."

Chapter 15
Blackout Protocol

Every new box, every shelf, every piece of paper recovered did little to answer any real questions, and instead created two or three more. Bradley was running thin on man power, and had long since run out of patience in determining what had been going on under his precinct and for how long. The officers he had working on the underground cavern, eight in total now, had been logging and organizing for hours and still they had no real solid clue of exactly what this space had been used for or by whom.

He brought down every battery powered light the precinct had, and even made a few calls to get other lights from other departments brought over to illuminate the huge space. And they hadn't even gotten to the strange train tracks yet. Bradley wanted to tell himself that this was simply part of an old abandoned city, maybe an old rail or subway station that had long since been forgotten. But the air coming from one of the tunnels didn't smell sour or old or forgotten.

Those tracks were still in use.

"Goeson! Give me a report!" He shouted to one of the forensic investigators, a portly man with a blonde goatee and sweat running down his face. He grabbed his tablet computer and marched over to Bradley, wiping his face on a handkerchief.

"So this is a real treat, Lieutenant," he smiled as he set the tablet down on a makeshift sawhorse. Bradley raised an eyebrow, and Officer Goeson cleared his throat. "Anyway, these crates are old, but not World War old, more like twenty to thirty years old, maybe a bit older. The files and papers I've started sorting, just by looking at them, have been so heavily redacted it'll be hard to get anything off them at all, but I have my ways.

"Oh and the shelves, the shelves had some old vials, completely used, and the labels have worn down too much to read, but I was able to get a little sediment from whatever liquid used to be there, so once I get that to the lab I might be able to tell what was in them to begin with."

He flashed a self satisfied grin at Bradley, who simply continued to peer at the man.

"So you're telling me we don't know much."

"We know very little if *anything* that they were doing down here, whoever *they* might be. Or might have been. But, one thing is super clear."

"And that one thing is?"

"They left in a hurry," he pointed to the train track. "Probably via those tunnels. Wherever those lead. But, and here's another thing, we can't find any plans at all in any database the city has, or the county, or the state of those tracks ever being built. Whoever built this place didn't want to leave a record that the public could find."

Bradley breathed in deep and slow and let out a grunt. He grimaced at the tracks in a distance, then at the other officers who were still working on sorting the mess. He shook his head and nodded his thanks to Officer Goeson.

"Keep filtering out anything you can make sense of. If you find anything worth noting, I want you to…" he stopped mid sentence as a breeze suddenly wafted through the cavern. The ground below them gently trembled, dust and pebbles and broken pieces of brick vibrated on the concrete.

Page 166

Then came a soft noise, no more than a whisper at first, until it grew louder, but just barely, as if it were a toy train that ran around a Christmas tree, no bigger than a house cat. A bright light grew in one end of the tunnel, and everyone watched with an intent gaze.

"Uhh, Lieutenant?" Officer Goeson said.

"I see it," Bradley replied.

A train came speeding out of the tunnel, far more silent than it should have been, as it raced along the track. Car after car sped by, and Bradley could just barely make out the blur of human figures inside the cars as they went. Then it was gone. Paper rustled on the shelves and floor from the wind drag of the speeding train, and not a few of the stacks that had been organized now fluttered in the air.

"Get me the mayor," Bradley said quietly.

———————

Donovan looked around the large room that housed the massive sphere. He drew near but wouldn't dare touch the thing, since he wasn't exactly sure what it was, or where it came from.

"So, what exactly are you?" He asked.

"I am the Joint Operations Neural Analysis Hub," the sphere replied. "J.O.N.A.H. for short. I'm a quantum computing, artificial intelligence that is capable of storing and processing petabytes of data."

"Uh huh, data on what?"

"I was programmed to oversee Blindsight," Jonah said. "You and I worked extensively together for a time."

"Don't you r-remember, General?" Joe cut in.

"I don't," Donovan said flatly.

"You don't what?" Jonah asked.

"I don't remember. I don't remember working with you, or Joe, or the crazy redhead that tried to kill me. Or the guy at the motel. I don't remember any of this. Joe told me I'd find the answers here. So…"

"Most interesting. Joe said that, did he?" Jonah asked, a bit of mirth in his computerized voice.

"Yes, yes he did. Tell him!" Donovan turned to Joe, who merely smiled back at him. "Go on. Tell him what you think I'm supposed to remember. All my specialties."

Joe didn't answer.

"Most interesting indeed," Jonah said.

"Sir, I've been able to recover some of the video from the corrupted files," the analyst said over his shoulder to Miller. Miller immediately ran over to him and leaned over his chair to peer at the screen.

"Show me," he said, putting the handset down, Jonah still on the other line. The analyst opened the same file as before and pressed play. "That can't be right," Miller said.

"That's the guy. Jacob Erst." The video dropped a few frames, but kept playing in sync with the audio. Miller scratched his head as he watched.

"What am I not getting here," he said. "That man isn't named Jacob."

"Joe here said you have the answers, Jonah," Donovan said as he paced back and forth in front of the large sphere.

"That depends," Jonah replied.

"On?"

"On what your questions are."

Page 168

"Ok, how about this for starters?" Donovan held up the small chip he had pulled from his neck. "I've been getting massive headaches anytime I did... whatever it is I can do. Then I found this in the back of my neck. As soon as I pulled it out, *bam,* headaches are gone. Can you explain that?"

"Psychic inhibitor implant," Jonah said plainly. When Donovan didn't reply, Jonah continued. "It was designed to monitor and contain psychic abilities. A fail-safe, you might say. To keep you, and others like you, under control. The headaches are the negative response to using your abilities. Apparently it didn't work, because you were able to not only unlock your abilities, but use them quite effectively. Next question."

Donovan looked at the tiny chip, then shook his head and dropped it to the floor. He stomped on it until there was a satisfying crunch.

"My memories," he continued. "Joe said you can return my memories. Make me remember everything."

"I cannot." Donovan sighed as the machine whirred softly. "That is, I cannot in my current state. After the incident, I was locked out of most Blindsight data. Until that is restored, I can do very little to help you."

"Ok, how do we restore that?" Donovan asked. Joe suddenly approached Donovan eagerly.

"He c-c-can help you remember," he said. "Just do what he as-as-asks."

"Sure, whatever. As long as it helps me figure this all out. Just, tell me what to do."

A panel on one part of the sphere slid open with a soft hiss, and a computer screen and keyboard slid out.

"It's possible that I can help," Jonah said. "But my liaison must reenable my access to the main database."

"Okaaaay, where do I find your liaison?"

"That would be you, of course," Jonah said flatly.

"That's nonsense. I've never been any kind of..." Donovan approached the screen and stopped mid-sentence. "Wait, this looks familiar. I recognize this." He stared at his own reflection in the glass screen. A single cursor softly blinked on the blank screen. Then he saw Kathy standing behind him.

He quickly turned, but of course she wasn't there. He looked at the screen again, she was there, but she looked different. Something about her hair, maybe? Or her clothes. He'd never seen her wear those clothes before. And a lab coat.

"General," Jonah said softly.

"I. There's something.. about this," Donovan said as he pressed his forefinger to a small pad next to the keyboard. Suddenly a red laser fanned out from somewhere near the screen. It scanned up and down over his face, over his right eye, then shut off. The screen came alive, as words flashed across it.

    Identity Confirmed.
    Biometric Key Accepted.
    Welcome Back General Jacob Orletta
Erst.

"Thank you, General," Jonah said, "for restoring my prime directives." Lights flashed all over the computer and the screen and keyboard retreated back inside the sphere.

"*General* Jacob Orletta Erst?" Donovan asked to no one. "Jacob... Orletta... Erst... J.O.E." Donovan spun on his heels to face Joe. "Joe, you're a general too?"

"I'm *the* general," Joe said plainly.

"But why did it need my…" Donovan froze, his eyes widened. He looked to the large computer sphere, then back to Joe. It hit him hard. "You… you didn't fight Pyotr. You didn't give the cops any identification at the checkpoint. You didn't help me lift that car on the highway. But… you fought the crazy redhead, the bad lady, in the lab." Donovan reached out a shaking hand towards Joe's shoulder. Joe didn't bother to move, and Donovan passed right through him, like grasping at air.

"Joe? What the hell are you?" He asked.

"I'm you, General," Joe said with a smile. "Always have been."

"What do you mean, sir?" Asked the analyst.

"That man," Miller thrust his finger against the computer screen, "is Donovan O'Connell. That's the man we've been tracking for days now."

"According to these files he's," the analyst double checked quickly before giving Miller his attention again. "General Jacob Erst, United States Marine Corp. Looks like he was a specialist in intelligence and snatched up by…" the analyst looked visibly shocked. "The CIA snatched him up. Everything here is really heavily redacted after that, but there's dozens of audio and video files with his name on them. And something called, 'Blindsight'."

"Find everything. I want to know what his role was, what he was doing, I want everything you can dig up. All of you. New focus is diving into this man's life. I want to know exactly what they were doing here," Miller said, as he pressed the mute button on the phone and went back to the handset.

"Tell me what you know about Jacob Erst," he said.

"I can do better than that," Jonah replied. "Would you like to see?"

Donovan sat on the floor with his knees pulled to his chest as his eyes shot left to right, his mind an absolute spiral of confusion and thoughts and images. Joe squatted down next to him.

"You okay, General?" He asked.

"What do you care?" Donovan shot back. "You're not even real."

"Eh, technically I am. I'm you. Well, you're me, actually. But who's splitting hairs here?"

"What did you bring me here for?" Donovan looked up at the thing that called itself Jonah. "I still don't remember everything."

"Perhaps I wasn't clear," Jonah said. "After the incident, I was locked out of the mainframe. As liaison to the intelligence community, my primary functions were at your control. Only your biometric data could clear that, and reset my main systems."

"What incident? What did I do here?"

"The incident involved an altercation between Siobhan Donaldson and yourself. The White Sands facility was compromised when a controlled detonation damaged the facility, and killed most the staff and test subjects."

"A controlled…" Donovan thought back to the lab, the scorched walls, the burnt files, the broken everything. The blood smearing the walls. "She did that?"

"*We* did that, well some of it," Joe cut in."

"Wait… *I* did that?!"

"Only some of it. While you were fighting her. She has a... bad temper," Joe made a face and leaned against the sphere while he picked his teeth.

"After the incident you locked me out of the mainframe, and I was unable to restart the program. But now, thanks to you, I can now resume my programmed directives uninhibited. In human terms, I am free."

"Would you at least tell me what that all means?"

"My prime directive is to see the project through to completion. Blindsight must continue. As to your lost memories, I am unable to tap into your brain and remove your blockage, in the same way you removed mine. Unfortunately, no one can do that, except you."

Joe reached behind his head and rubbed the back of his neck. "You took it out. You can remember now."

"The inhibitor thing? That was keeping me from remembering?"

"Not exactly," Jonah answered. "It was keeping you from accessing the full extent of your abilities. With it removed, you should have no problem undoing what you did in the first place."

"Which means?"

"What you have done for me, you can do for yourself," Jonah replied. A side door in the room suddenly slid open, revealing a small but exquisitely clean bathroom. There was a toilet, sink, and mirror inside and nothing else. Driven by sheer curiosity Donovan stood up and moved to inspect it. Both Jonah and Joe were silent.

"Thanks, but I don't really have to go," Donovan said, then caught a glimpse of himself in the mirror. It was only in his peripheral vision, but he saw his own reflection, move. He whipped his head around and stared intently, but nothing happened. Then as he looked away, it happened again. He paid more attention to it this time, noting that instead of looking in the opposite direction, like a reflection would do, it looked directly *at* him.

Without a word he stepped into the bathroom, braced his hands on the sink, and stared intently at himself in the mirror. He turned his head left and right while keeping the main focus on his own face. Nothing changed.

Until it did.

He leaned in closer to the mirror, having seen something shift, but only in the reflection of his eye. First he squinted, then he opened his eyes wide, neither caused a repeat of the illusion. He blinked, and Joe was standing behind him in the mirror, only when he looked over his shoulder, the "Joe" he had been traveling with, or thought he had, wasn't there. Only the mirrored version.

"I'm you, always have been," Joe repeated.

"But the truck," Donovan whispered.

"Delivered and arranged by me," Jonah said from the main room. "Don't you remember the phone call with your 'lawyer'? When I told you to find the truck and get out of the building? It was easy enough to have a vehicle delivered."

"The car accident. You moved that—"

"No, General," Joe interrupted. "*You* did. Well, we did if you want to get technical."

"I still don't understand." Donovan stared at Joe in the mirror, apparently having a conversation with himself. Until suddenly Joe changed. It was subtle, but noticeable. His face altered just enough to be different than it had been. Then he slowly got taller, like a bean sprout caught on a time lapse camera might show. His balding head grew hair, no, the hair didn't grow, it just appeared. Donovan's jaw dropped. Moment by moment, Joe began to look more and more like himself.

"*Patient Interview Jacob Orletta Erst, day fifty-two,*" a man's voice played in the main room, drawing Donovan's attention.

"*How are you feeling today, General Erst?*" The man said.

"*I told you, that's not my name. Why do you keep calling me that?*" The new voice was unmistakably Donovan. His jaw dropped as he listened.

"*What would you prefer I call you?*" The doctor asked.

"*How about my name? I told you again and again, I am* General *Donovan O'Connell.*" The recording said. Jonah suddenly cut it off.

"What was that?" Donovan asked without leaving the bathroom.

"That was day fifty-two of your experimental treatments," Jonah replied. "You were curious about what was being done at Blindsight, and subjected yourself to the experiments, under the care of Dr. Kathleen Penner," Jonah said.

"Kathy," Donovan looked back in the mirror. There she was, standing next to the hyperbaric chamber as Donovan lay inside, an oxygen mask over his face, yet he smiled at her and held up a hand to the glass. Donovan blinked and he now saw Kathy injecting herself with a compound, whilst looking over her shoulder. No one could see, except for the security cameras overhead.

"I watched her experiment on herself. She developed mild abilities of telekinesis, but you, General, you developed abilities and so much more. You developed an alter ego," Jonah said. "While General Erst could lift a tank with his mind, General *O'Connell* could do much, much more."

Page 175

"The *specialties* were fun," the mirror O'Connell said, in Joe's voice, "but I'd really like my body back now."

"This… this isn't happening. None of this is real. It's all just in my head," Donovan said, leaning over the sink as though he might be sick.

"Exactly," Jonah said with a sudden excitement. "It *is* all in your head. A very unforeseen outcome to the experiments! Don't you see, General? Jacob developed some extraordinary abilities, but you, *you* developed another life. The perfect specimen. The whole reason Blindsight was started in the first place. Imagine an asset that could switch personalities at will, and with it unlock unheard of psychic potential, then shut it all off and be impervious to the deepest of interrogations! You are the perfect sleeper agent."

"You're telling me I, we, whoever did this to me on purpose? That I'm just some experiment?" Donovan was getting agitated with each passing moment. "That I injured and killed those people in the casino as part of a government program or something?!"

"No, don't worry, O'Connell," Joe said, placing a hand on Donovan's shoulder. "You didn't hurt those people. I did."

"You did?!"

"Who could have known that the hypnotist would trigger a switch in your personalities. Another unforeseen event, but quite an interesting study," Jonah said. "Still, yes it was you, Jacob, that initiated the Blackout Protocol that set our experiment in motion. Neither you, nor I thought the Donovan ego would go rogue, as it were."

"Blackout Protocol?" Donovan was nearly shaking with anger as he asked.

"Psychically blacking out the part of your ego that is Jacob Erst, the real you, in favor of the alter ego, Donovan

O'Connell. Unfortunately, by this time Kathleen and Donovan had a plan of their own, to shut down Blindsight and disappear. You used your biometric access as a government liaison to lock me down. That will no longer be an option, however," Jonah said in a somewhat menacing tone.

Donovan turned on Joe, or at least his mental projection of Joe, who switched back and forth between the Joe he knew and the image of himself like a glitching computer screen.

"So why did you bring me here? Why did you kill Kathy? Why did you do this to me?"

"*You* brought you here, Donovan," Joe said. "You wanted answers. You're the one that locked Jonah out, and ran away with Kathy in the first place. You've been playing with *my* body for the better part of four years. That wasn't part of the deal."

"If you created me, and you gave me free reign, what did you think would happen? I'm not some killer. That's you!"

"Wrong, that's *us*!" Joe shouted. "You don't have to remember Afghanistan. You don't have to remember Iran! You got to run away and live the little civilian life, and forget everything we did! Everything *I* did. But it's my body, my mind, and *my* power!"

Donovan began to protest, when suddenly he was flung across the room, several feet into the air, and slammed his back against the concrete wall, knocking the air out of his lungs. He fell back to the floor and crumbled, gasping for breath.

"Perhaps it is time to take your internal feud elsewhere," Jonah said, the AI speaking more calmly. "I have alerted the authorities of your presence. They will be here soon to collect you, unless you leave."

Page 177

Donovan stood up with some effort, cradling his ribs as he regained his composure. "You're a murderer. A psychopath. I'm in charge now, *Jacob*." Joe glowered at Donovan as the pair faced off against one another.

"You *are* me," Joe retorted. "You don't get to run away this time, General."

"Who said I'm running?" Donovan raised a hand to his forehead and closed his eyes. "Everything I was, everything I did, go away now." He whispered.

"You can't…"

"Everything I was, everything I did, go away now," Donovan repeated.

"Donovan… listen to me…" Joe tried to shout, but his voice grew quieter and quieter.

"I'll pay for it all. But everything I was, I'm not anymore. I'm not that anymore. I won't be that anymore."

Joe was screaming, shouting, throwing his hands in the air, but no sound came out, and no effect followed his tantrums.

"Interesting," Jonah said softly, making note of the entire event.

"Everything… I… *was*…" tears streamed down Donovan's face. He opened his eyes slowly. Joe was gone. Swallowing hard, Donovan turned his face to the machine, the lights flickering softly, the cameras facing him. "Goodbye, Jonah," Donovan said.

"Goodbye, General O'Connell," Jonah said, in his most robotic sounding voice yet. Donovan turned towards the door, as it opened for him. Without looking back he treaded down the long hallway, the lights coming on before him and turning off after him. The inclinator ride was silent, peaceful, as he made his way back up the five long stories towards the lobby.

He closed his eyes, and thought of Kathy, of their life together, of the four years that seemed like a lifetime, and he smiled. He wasn't sure what the future held for him next, but he was ready for it regardless. As the inclinator door opened, he opened his eyes, and his heart stopped.

"Hello, General," Meredith said. Then fire filled the doorway and surrounded Donovan.

Chapter 16
Specialties

Agent Miller had stepped gingerly through the several holes in the concrete walls to get to the train track behind them all. He was sure there had been an easier way to reach the tracks, but he hadn't been able to find it, so this was the next best option. When he asked Jonah how the holes came to be, he had only told him there had been a scuffle. Given what Miller knew about the nature of these individuals, and the scorch marks all over the laboratory they had found, he wasn't so sure he wanted to know the details of such a scuffle.

"Are you sure this is a good idea?" One of the analysts asked him as he stood by the tracks.

"No," Miller said honestly. "You all keep at what you're doing, I want a full report when I get back."

If I get back.

"How long do you think you'll be gone?"

"I can't answer that. But if this guy has the information I'm looking for, it shouldn't be that long at all. Just keep doing what you're doing, sorting, logging, making sense of all this, and I'll return as soon as I can." The analyst nodded and slowly and carefully treaded back through the holes in the walls toward the main lab. In truth, Miller didn't know if he could trust this Jonah character, but he wanted answers, and this guy seemed to have them.

A rush of wind from one of the tunnels blew Miller's hair back in dramatic fashion, and the ground slightly shook. His phone buzzed in his pocket and he quickly answered.

"Agent Miller, FBI," he tried to sound as professional as he could.

"Get on the train, it'll take you to the rendezvous point. Once you get there, ask for Jennifer, she will direct you where you need to go," Jonah said over the phone.

"Okay. Tell me again that I can trust you," Miller answered, trying to sound confident through his suddenly dry throat and mouth.

"My only interest was subduing Jacob Erst, as you saw from the videos," Jonah sounded somewhat saddened suddenly. "To that end I believe I've succeeded. What happens next is entirely up to you, Agent Miller. And the FBI of course. However, please understand that what you're going to see is so top secret, the majority of Congress doesn't know it exists. And that's for good reason."

"In that case I'll be meeting you soon," Miller said, as he hung up the call. No sooner did he replace the phone in his pocket than the train pulled out of the tunnel and came to a stop directly in front of him. He sighed.

"Here goes nothing."

Her wicked smile quickly turned into a look of surprise and shock as Meredith was flung back through the air and landed hard on her tailbone. She grimaced at the pain and turned her face quickly to Donovan, who stepped out of the inclinator doors completely unscathed. He gave her a look like a father might give a child who just got caught with a face full of chocolate chip cookies and knew they were in trouble.

"Enough, Siobhan," Donovan said. "Can't we just talk a minute?"

"So you remember me now, do you?" Meredith said, as she got to her feet and kicked off her heels, dropping her height by a few inches.

"I remember more than I'd like to," Donovan replied.

"In that case, Joe, shall we continue where we left off?" Meredith smirked and opened her palm, causing her entire hand to burst into flames.

"No," Donovan shook his head, "I'm afraid Jacob won't be joining us. Not for a long time if I have anything to say about it. You can talk to *me*, though."

"That's no fun," Meredith tossed her hand casually outward, and the flame jumped like a thrown ball towards Donovan, who batted it away with a lethargic wave of his hand.

"You murdered all those people in the White Sands lab," Donovan lowered his eyebrows. "I stopped you then, I'll stop you now."

"You're one to talk, General. Your body count is higher than the rest of us put together!" Meredith grunted and threw more fire his way, and Donovan caught them like soft balls and extinguished each with a clench of his fist. "*People* is a kind word for those monsters anyway," Meredith spat as she threw another easily dodged fireball. "Those *people* did this to me, to so many others, and you just stood by and let them!" Another fireball. Another block.

"You volunteered for the program. It's not like they dragged you off the street. You're just as complicit in this as they were," Donovan began to slowly march forward, closing a fist as his fingers crawled with blue electric worms. He quickly opened his hand and the lightning jerked and twitched from his hand across the floor in a jigsaw pattern towards Meredith. She leapt to the side as it snaked up from the floor like a growing tree with a loud crack and flashed a moment before vanishing again.

"And what about you?" She shrieked. "What about your disappearing act? You just walked away with that talentless whore like none of us meant anything to you!"

"I warned you before… don't talk about Kathy that way," Donovan lowered his head and glared at her through his hooded eyes.

"No? You and Kathy made your escape in the chaos and carnage. As much as you'd like to blame Joe for that, it wasn't him who left. It was you, O'Connell!"

"I left, but… I needed to put and end to it. I didn't kill anyone though. *That* was Joe. That wasn't me."

"You *are* Joe!" Meredith tossed her hands left and right like a boxer throwing jabs. Fire flew across the room and Donovan was forced to side step a few of the wild flames. He finally pressed his palm out and the telekinetic push knocked Meredith off her balance.

"Not anymore! I'll atone for what I did. But this chaotic feud you have with me has to end," he lifted his palm upward and Meredith raised off the floor, her arms caught at her sides with invisible binds.

"You faked your death once, General, this time I'll make it permanent!" Meredith closed her eyes tightly, then opened them wide as they went red with flame, her hair ignited, her entire body began to immolate, even her clothes lit and began to burn.

Donovan dropped her to the floor and placed both hands against his temples and lowering his face, looked at Meredith over his eyebrows. He glared intently and she froze.

"Don't make me do it," he warned.

"You wouldn't. You wouldn't do that to me," she swallowed hard.

"I would. Please. Please don't make me," Donovan watched her intently.

"If I go, we all go. Everyone in this place, you, me, this whole station goes down. I'll do it," the flames grew larger as her jacket fell to the floor, still burning.

"No, not this time you won't." Donovan squinted and peered through the growing blaze into Meredith's burning eyes. She gasped, but he held her gaze. She tried to look away but he wouldn't let her. The fire sputtered as he began to sweat, but he refused to look away, to lose his concentration, or even blink.

The fire extinguished with a loud whooshing sound.

Meredith's eyes rolled back in her head and she began to fall to the floor. Donovan reached out one hand, even from a distance, and caught her telekinetically. She glided motionless across the floor toward him until she was in his arms. Most her clothes were scorched but she was clothed enough. He cradled her in his arms as she lay limp.

"I'm sorry, Siobhan," he whispered. "I'll look after you, and I'll make this right. I promise."

As he carried her unconscious body towards the tracks, he spotted a man in a wool suit standing on the platform with his hands in his pockets. His hair was short and very neatly combed, and he had a leather shoulder bag slung across his body. Donovan approached slowly, but confidently, as though he was supposed to be there.

"Nice day," the man said.

"It is. Really nice," Donovan replied, still holding Siobhan in his arms. The man glanced over, then down at the unconscious woman and back up at Donovan, before returning his eyes to the tracks.

"Rough day at the office?" He asked.

"You have no idea," Donovan said, as he swallowed hard. The man chuckled.

"Where you headed?"

"I'm… uh, East. Just East of here."

"Nice. Where from?" The man looked over again, then smiled. "I'm sorry, it's my nature. I'm a, well *was* a journalist. I guess it's still habit to ask too many questions," the man said and stuck out his hand. "Elliot Kane," he looked at Donovan's full arms and retracted his hand awkwardly.

"I'm… Donovan. Nice to meet you Elliot. My partner and I were working on a project in," he cleared his throat, "… in New Mexico. She's hard on the bottle sometimes," he laughed nervously.

"Oh I get it. My former partner was the same," He smiled and the two stood awkwardly for a full minute, but to Donovan it felt like a year. Finally, Elliot spoke again. "If you're headed East, it's none of my business but, you might try Montauk. It's over there on platform five. Just take the third rail and you'll get there on time," he cleared his throat and smiled. Donovan looked to where he was pointing and nodded.

"Right, stupid me. I get this place mixed up all the time," he said as he turned to head in the other direction.

"Oh I get it, yeah. It was nice meeting you, Donovan. And your partner there," Elliot smiled and wave, as Donovan nodded and briskly headed for the other platform.

No sooner did he approach the platform, then the tracks rumbled and a train arrived on the third rail. He gave one last look over his shoulder, but Elliot was gone. With a shrug, he stepped into the open doors and laid Siobhan on one bench, then sat down opposite her on another.

"So, Montauk it is," he said to her. "Ever been there, Siobhan? No? Me neither. Where have you been I wonder?"

As the doors closed and the train began to move, he leaned forward to rest on his knees and turn his gaze on the unconscious woman before him. Placing his fingers on both temples he allowed his focus to drift as he reached into the recesses of her mind. Meredith had answers he needed, and in return, he'd tried to quell her burning anger.

Heh, fiery inside and out.

Chapter 17
Brand New Day

Lieutenant Bradley trudged up the stairs from the basement just in time to see his officers lined on one side of the bullpen while a small army of men and women in nondescript suits and clothing packed up every file, computer and piece of evidence on Donovan O'Connell. His head spun and his anger fumed at what he saw, and if he had had his coffee in hand he might have thrown it.

"Just what the hell do you think you're doing?!" He bellowed in his normal, booming tone. "Who the hell do you think you are?"

A man in round, wireframe glasses, wearing a more expensive version of the black suit some of the other men were wearing, moved so swiftly to head off Bradley that he thought the man had floated on air. He stuck out a big hand and took Bradley's so firmly that he was caught off guard a moment.

"Deputy Director Nichols of the Central Intelligence Agency," the man said loud enough for all to hear. "You've done fine work here, Lieutenant Bradley, fine work." His voice dipped to a lower volume and almost seemed to drip with secrecy. "Between you and me, and the agency, I don't think anyone has handled this little, lapse, better than you have. We're in your debt, and that's a debt worth having."

Bradley glared.

"You wanna tell me what the CIA is doing in my precinct taking my evidence on my suspect?" Nichols' smile twisted and he gripped Bradley's hand harder. Bradley gripped back as both men tried to assert their dominance.

"This is way above your pay grade, Lieutenant," Nichols hissed. "Your *suspect* is a long time asset of the agency, and as such we are confiscating any trace that he was ever here. Your precinct has been condemned, due to unsafe working conditions related to your basement. You, and your officers will be moved to a newer," Nichols glanced around, "*cleaner* facility post haste. And I suspect there's a promotion in there for you as well." Nichols grinned. "How's Captain sound?"

"And what of mister Parker?" Bradley raised an eyebrow. "The so called Homeland agent? Will he be moving to our new facility as well, so we can continue *that* investigation? Or is the agency taking him off our hands?"

"Who?" Nichols smiled. "I'm so glad we understand each other, Captain." Then he added, "It is *Captain* Bradley now, isn't it? You tell me."

Bradley sighed. He had been around long enough to know that this was a fight he wasn't going to win. If he was being honest with himself, he didn't want to win this fight either. Since Donovan O'Connell had shown up in his city, everything went haywire in his world. Maybe it was for the best that it was being taken out of his hands. He released Nichols' hand and nodded as he looked around his bullpen.

"Listen up!" He bellowed. "Give these fine ladies and gentlemen your full cooperation. Gather your things quickly and quietly and meet outside in fifteen minutes. We're moving to a new precinct." Stunned by the announcement the officers looked at each other but didn't budge. "Let's get to it, people!" The bullpen came alive, and Bradley felt a firm hand on his shoulder.

"I knew I could count on you, Captain," Nichols said.

"Thank you for all your help, Deputy Director. We'll be out of your hair shortly." Bradley smiled the same smile he had practiced over years in the force. It was the cordial smile that he grew well used to using to superiors when he knew he was outmatched, or told to do something he didn't particularly want to do. Even now, with retirement on the horizon, he still had to use that professional smile that said he understood his orders, even when he was screaming inside to tell them off.

Bradley quickly and quietly made his way to his office, shut the door, and began pretending to pack while he slipped an earpiece into his ear and hit the speed dial for Agent Miller's phone. He took his time gathering a single paper at a time and stacking them neatly into one corner while the phone rang and rang. After one failed attempt, he tried again.

"Come on, Miller. Answer your damn phone," he growled quietly to himself. The line picked up.

"Brad... I don't... much service. I'm underground... train going... someone named Jonah..." Miller's voice broke up every few words but Bradley got the gist.

"The CIA is here and they're taking everything. Did you find O'Connell?" He whispered through his teeth, not sure who might be watching or listening.

"O'Connell? No, no! It's... else... whole thing has... been chasing... wrong guy!"

"The wrong guy? What do you mean?"

"I'll have to... you in when I see... just got to wherever this train..." The call died. Bradley gritted his teeth and hung up his end, then had an idea. He moved over to his cabinet and opened the doors, grabbed the decanter and slowly poured himself a drink. He looked down to where he knew the camera was, the one he found and left a while ago.

Page 191

"I know you're listening. I know you can see this. I just want you to know I'm not done with you. I'll figure this out, and when I do, I'm coming for you. You hear me?" Bradley took a drink and swallowed hard. "I'm coming for you."

Agent Miller gingerly stepped out of the train car and peered around from left to right, then up and down. He'd never seen anything like this place. The ceiling looked as though it were open to the blue sky, but just beyond the projection, or hologram, was definitely more steel and concrete. He figured he had to still be deep underground, but exactly where in the country he was, he had no clue.

The was a large turntable to his left, and multiple tunnels and tracks that disappeared into the darkness, same as the tunnel he had come from. Obviously this was some kind of transit hub.

He caught a red light in his peripheral vision, and jerked his head to look just as a laser seemed to fan over his person and move up and down his face a few times. The light vanished, and he jumped when a voice shook him.

"Can I help you?" Jennifer smiled and said.

"Hi… I'm Agent Miller of the FBI," he pulled his badge and nearly dropped it, his hands shook when he tried to show it to the woman. Jennifer giggled.

"What can I do for you, Agent Miller?"

"I'm looking for a man… he told me to find Jennifer. Are you Jennifer?"

"I sure am! What man told you to find me?"

"His name is… uh… it's, Jonah."

"Oh my golly gosh he's quite popular today. You just missed another man and woman who paid Jonah a visit earlier today. Now, what you're going to want to do is head just over this way to the inclinators. Take the one on the right, that's our right, like stage right, not proper right, and head down to the farthest sub-level, B5. B, like bee. Got that?" Jennifer smiled and lifted her tablet as she tapped and made notes.

"I think so. Elevator on the right."

"Inclinator. Don't take the elevator. You won't like where that goes," Jennifer laughed, snorted, and pushed her glasses up her nose. Miller smiled and quickly took his leave, speed walking over to the two doors the strange woman had said.

Agent Miller was a professional, trained at Quantico after serving seven years with the LAPD. He had been plucked off his unit by a Federal headhunter, who apparently had been watching his career from the beginning. After ten years with the Bureau, he had seen some things. But nothing had prepared him for what this case had shown him.

A man that can move things with his mind, a woman that controls fire, and underground laboratories and bunkers he was certain the Bureau, at least no one with his clearance level, knew existed. Now he was in the midst of it, with no backup, no oversight, and no approval from his superiors. In fact, no one but the analysts even knew that he left the site, and no one, not even himself, knew exactly where he was.

He took the inclinator down five stories until he came to the long dark hallway. Lights came alive as he walked, until he came to the large metal doors at the end of the way. They parted for him without barely a sound.

"There you are," Jonah said, from seemingly everywhere and nowhere in particular. Miller's jaw dropped as he entered the room and stood before the great sphere.

"What in the hell…" he whispered.

"Pleased to meet you in person, Agent Miller. I'm Jonah."

"*You're* Jonah?!"

"I am. I know this is a lot to process, however before we begin I'm afraid I need your help."

"What do you need me for?" Miller stepped closer to get a better look at the massive machine.

"My programming states I must be tethered, partnered with, a liaison from the United States. For security reasons, of course. Ideally this would be a member of the intelligence community. Previously that was General Jacob Erst, of the CIA, whom you've come to know as Donovan O'Connell. However, I'm in need of a new partner, as it were." A panel slid quietly open and a computer screen and keyboard, with a small fingerprint pad next to it, slid out quietly.

"I see," Miller said, walking over to the open panel. "So this is how it was done," he scoffed and shook his head. "I'm guessing if I want answers, all I have to do is sign on the bottom line, is that right?"

"More than answers," Jonah hummed. "Progress."

"Progress?" Miller looked at the screen as it came alive with video surveillance footage, both old and new, rosters of dozens of assets, and locations around the United States of additional laboratories. Miller's eyes widened.

"Welcome to Blindsight, Agent Miller."

Donovan stared intently at the unconscious woman laying on the bench across from his. Voices and scenes and images played out in near opaque visions before his lazy eyes, none of them making much sense, as he focused on the recesses of Siobhan's mind. He remembered he had done this sort of thing many times over, usually with terrorists but sometimes with politicians or heads of state as well. Whomever had information the CIA wanted, "the General" was sent in to get it.

He remembered he taught a select few to do the same, but none of his test subjects ever achieved the level of control he had. Telepathy truly was one of his many specialties.

He remembered how it felt, how the dreams would plague him for weeks afterwards, when he looked into another person's mind. People don't think in straight lines, or in nice orderly fashion. They usually don't think in video, but in garbled words from multiple conversations. They think of images, and *feelings* and everything that shouldn't be able to be easily read. Because it's not.

He remembered those feelings. Joy over a newborn's birth, or suffering over the loss of one. Anger at a betrayal, or love for a wife. It was no wonder Jacob Erst developed an entirely different personality, in Donovan O'Connell. Perhaps it was a miracle that Donovan was the *only* other personality Jacob developed.

But the most amazing thing to Donovan, as he sat on that bench and tried to make sense of Siobhan's memories, in hopes of accessing his own, was that he *was remembering.* And to him, that was the best thing to happen to him in the last week. And the worst.

General Jacob Erst had been a monster. He was surprised Siobhan fell so head over heels in love with the man. On the other side of the coin, Donovan was a kind, compassionate person, who fell in love with Kathy. Donovan and Jacob, truly an embodiment of Dr. Jekyll and Mr. Hyde.

Suddenly, the train screeched to a halt, the sound scraping against Donovan's already frayed nerves. He gripped the armrest, his knuckles white, the air thick with the acrid tang of burnt metal and something else, something sterile, like antiseptic left too long in an open wound. Across from him, Siobhan slumped against the bench, her red hair matted with sweat, her breathing shallow but steady. She was still out cold, and had a bruise blooming on her temple from where he'd slammed her with a telekinetic burst when he had emerged from the inclinator.

He still regretted that.

Donovan looked to his right, half expecting to see Joe sitting on the bench not far from him, or passed out on the floor like usual when they had traveled together. But no, he wouldn't be there. In fact he had never been there. The sleeping man had been a figment of his split consciousness, stuttering and fighting to come back and assert control over this body.

Joe was gone. Receded deep somewhere into his mind, and Donovan didn't have any intention of inviting him back at any point in the near future. He had Siobhan now to help recover the fragments of his memory and piece together everything he had made himself forget.

The train doors hissed open, revealing a concrete platform bathed in harsh fluorescent light. He held up a hand in front of his face to block the harsh beams that cascaded into the train car. They had arrived at Camp Hero, Montauk.

The end of the line.

Donovan hauled Siobhan up, slinging her arm over his shoulder, her weight dragging against him like a sack of wet sand. He stepped out, the cold air biting at his exposed skin, his torn jacket flapping uselessly. But this platform wasn't empty.

Six armed guards in black tactical gear stood waiting, rifles at the ready, their faces obscured by visors that reflected the harsh lights. One guard stepped forward, lowering his weapon slightly. His visor tilted, and Donovan caught a glimpse of wide eyes behind it.

"General Erst?" the guard said, voice cracking with something like awe. "Sir, is that you?" Donovan froze, his pulse hammering in his throat. General Erst. The name hit like a punch, stirring those jagged memory shards. Desert sands, concrete domes, screams in a lab. Whoever this was, he knew Donovan from a time before *Blindsight*. The guard's reaction was a lifeline. It was genuine. He could use it.

He straightened, forcing his voice to steady, channeling the authority he'd seen in those fleeting visions of himself in a uniform.

"It sure is," he said, meeting the guard's gaze. "I've got an escapee from the *Blindsight* project. White Sands was compromised, so here we are."

The guards exchanged glances, their rifles shifting slightly. The lead guard tilted his head, confusion seeping into his tone.

"Blindsight? Sir, I don't... what project?" Donovan's gut twisted, but he kept his face hard, unyielding.

"You heard me. She's one of ours. Dangerous. She's a pyrokinetic. Get her to sick bay, under guard, now," he grunted as best he could manage.

The guard hesitated, then nodded sharply. "Yes, sir." He gestured to two others, who moved forward, grabbing Siobhan's limp form. She groaned as they dragged her away,

Page 197

her heels scraped against the concrete, leaving faint streaks of dirt. Donovan watched her disappear through a steel door, a knot tightening in his chest. He didn't trust these guards, didn't trust this place, but he'd bought himself time.

Maybe.

"The hell is going on here?" Came a rough, aged voice from behind the guards. "We aren't expecting any deliveries today."

"It's uh, General Erst, sir. He's... he's come back." The first guard stammered to the unseen voice.

"Come back?!"

Donovan started to speak, to put on the act, but he froze, his eyes widened, and his throat closed. Lieutenant Bradley, hobbled around the guards on a bum leg and stood before Donovan. His hair was white, there were more wrinkles in his face, and he looked to have lost fifty pounds or so. Donovan looked at him in confusion.

"Lieutenant—"

"Colonel," Bradley's powerful voice even sounded older, but still just as strong.

"Right... Colonel," Donovan swallowed hard.

"O'Connell," Bradley grunted, and smiled wide. "I've been waiting a long time for you."

Preview:
"The Third Rail"

"Hit me," Elliot said as he hunched over the bar, his chin rested on his wrist, and his arms crossed on the worn wood that had seen it's fair share of drunks.

"I think you've had enough," the bartender said, as he leaned in towards Elliot. "Go home, Elliot. Get some rest. Things will be better tomorrow."

"Tomorrow, heh. Just a word without meaning without form or shape or substance or meaning. What even *is* tomorrow, eh Patrick?" Elliot sat up straight with some effort and tried to stand from the barstool. "Time is a construct. A cage and we're all canaries chirping for seeds and… and…" he looked down at his empty wrist. "And watches. Where's my watch?"

He stumbled and tripped over his own heel and careened backwards. But before hitting the ground he was suddenly caught by a pair of strong arms. He was hoisted up onto his feet and steadied.

"Don't worry, Patrick, I'll see him home," came a gravely, deep voice. "Up you go, young man. Let's get you back home and to bed," the man said. Elliot allowed the stranger to duck under his armpit and carefully half carry him out of the bar.

The cold October air hit Elliot's face like a slap, momentarily sharpening the blurred edges of his vision. The neon sign for McGinty's buzzed and flickered behind them, casting pink and blue shadows across the wet pavement. Rain had fallen earlier, leaving the street slick and reflective, a mirror for the sodium vapor streetlights.

"I can walk," Elliot mumbled, though his legs suggested otherwise.

"Sure you can," the stranger said, his grip firm but not unkind. He was older, maybe sixty, with silver hair visible beneath a worn fedora. His coat smelled of cigarettes and something else, like printer's ink, maybe, or old paper. "But humor an old man, would you?"

They shuffled past a row of parked cars, their chrome bumpers catching the light. A taxi rolled by, its tires hissing on the wet asphalt. Somewhere in the distance, a siren wailed.

"I know you," Elliot said suddenly, squinting at the man's profile. "Don't I know you?"

"Maybe. I know you, Elliot Kane. Used to read your pieces in the Tribune before…" The man let the sentence hang there, delicate and unfinished.

Before.

Before the Carmichael story that never ran. Before Editor Bob Linton warned him it would be career suicide to pursue those leads. Before he did it anyway because no one told Elliot Kane what to do. Before the blacklist that wasn't official but might as well have been carved in stone.

"That was a lifetime ago," Elliot said.

"Six months," the stranger corrected. "But I suppose that's a lifetime in this business."

They stopped at the corner of Third and Lexington. The stranger shifted his weight, reaching into his coat with his free hand. When it emerged, he was holding a manila envelope, creased and dog-eared at the corners.

"My name's Henry Kovacs. I was a typesetter at the Tribune for thirty years. Retired now." He pressed the

envelope against Elliot's chest. "There's a story here. A real one. The kind you used to chase."

Elliot's fingers fumbled with the envelope, nearly dropping it before clutching it against his rumpled shirt. "I don't... I'm not—"

"You're a drunk," Kovacs said matter-of-factly. "But you're not dead. Not yet." He released Elliot's arm, steadying him with one hand on his shoulder. "Those are transit authority documents. Maintenance logs from the new subway extension. The numbers don't add up, and three inspectors who asked questions don't work there anymore. One of them doesn't work anywhere anymore, if you catch my meaning."

The fog in Elliot's mind began to clear, that old instinct stirring like something waking from hibernation.

"Why me?"

"Because you're the only one who'll look at it. The only one desperate enough or stubborn enough or drunk enough not to care about the consequences." Kovacs stepped back, tipping his hat. "Your apartment's two blocks that way. Think you can make it?"

Elliot nodded, gripping the envelope tighter.

"Good," Kovacs said, already turning to leave. "Read it when you're sober, Kane. And watch yourself. Whoever's behind this doesn't want no one to know what they're doing. In our line of work, that's exactly what needs be knowing."

Then he was gone, disappearing into the amber glow of the streetlights, leaving Elliot swaying on the corner with a manila envelope and the first stirring of something he hadn't felt in months.

Purpose.

Page 201

Additional Titles by D. Skvarek

Sapphire City

The Omega Archives: Exodus

The Omega Archives: Vernula Sun

The Timeless Zodiac series

www.ingramcontent.com/pod-product-compliance
Lightning Source LLC
Chambersburg PA
CBHW070748180626
46818CB00007B/3031